When would the magic come?

Aaron had another reason to go to the ravine. It was where he sat to try and find the quiet place inside himself where the magic dwelt. Once or twice he thought he actually did catch a touch of some deep power running through him. But it always vanished as soon as he became aware of it.

He stood gazing pensively into the ravine. Suddenly the deep silence was shattered by a screech. Aaron screamed. A hideous winged creature was swooping toward him. It was leather-skinned, twice the height of a man, with a wingspread like a house. As its knife-like talons stretched for his throat, its oddly human face leered with malevolent glee and it hissed "Come to me!"

Look for these other Bruce Coville titles from Scholastic:

Bruce Coville's Book of Monsters
Bruce Coville's Book of Aliens
Bruce Coville's Book of Ghosts
Bruce Coville's Book of Nightmares
Bruce Coville's Book of Spine Tinglers

and coming soon:

Bruce Coville's Book of Monsters II
Bruce Coville's Book of Aliens II

BRUCE COVILLE'S BOOK OF

Compiled and edited by
Bruce Coville

Illustrated by
John Pierard

A GLC Book

SCHOLASTIC INC.
New York Toronto London Auckland Sydney

ISBN: 0-590-25931-8

10 9 8 7 6 5 4 3 2 1 6 7 8 9/9 0/0

Printed in the U.S.A. 40

First Scholastic printing May 1996

For Daniel Weiss, one of this project's godfathers and a magician in his own right

CONTENTS

Contents

INTRODUCTION: CLOUDY, WITH A CHANCE OF MAGIC

I loved to watch magicians work when I was a kid. In fact, one of the highlights of my life was being called on stage one night when I was about eight to have silver dollars pulled from behind my ear.

Later, when I started hearing explanations of how magicians worked their various tricks, I convinced myself that these stories were just a cover. I preferred to believe that the best magicians really did know magic, and were just putting out the story that their tricks were mere "sleight of hand" so people wouldn't get upset and burn them at the stake or something.

The truth is, I still want to believe that, at least about the real killer tricks, the ones that still *feel* like magic to me. I don't want to think that every single thing in the world can be pinned down and explained. I prefer to have a little mystery left.

Which is not to say that I don't like sleight of hand for its own sake. In fact, for a while my brother and I bought tricks from a mail order magic catalog, and I loved learning how to do them. When I had a chance to visit a city (we were country boys) I would look for a magic shop. But much as I enjoyed the tricks, I always hoped I would stumble into a shop where they carried the real stuff.

I've been looking for magic all my life. The one place where I could always count on finding it was the library. This was a place filled with the work of magicians indeed, and the fantastical stories of Hugh Lofting, P. L. Travers, E. Nesbitt, and others did much to sate my hunger for magic.

Now, believing in magic (not to mention longing for it) seems to be fairly common among kids. But in their hurry to grow up, many young people tuck that longing away. It's as if they think that growing older—and supposedly wiser—means you must look at the world through more serious eyes. Such people forget that magic is often deadly serious.

As for me, I thought Peter Pan had the right idea. I was in no hurry to grow up, partly because I could see that I was having more fun than any of the grown-ups around me.

So I kept looking for magic.

That's why October remains my favorite month, and Halloween my favorite holiday. These are the times when it feels like magic is in the air, and wonders can be waiting just around the nearest corner.

Of course, a lot of things have magic in them. The natural world is filled with it, in everything from the majestic power of a great thunderstorm to the miracle of a caterpillar sprouting beautiful wings.

Reading and writing strike me as being magical, too. What an amazing thing: to take thoughts that are in my head, turn them into little black marks on paper, and have them re-created in your head!

But when it comes right down to it, I'm still looking for out-and-out magic, and for me, stories remain the best place to find it—stories that have wishes, and transformations, and miracles.

Stories, in fact, like the eleven you will find gathered in this collection.

If you, like me, are in search of magic, you've come to the right place, because we've got a bookful of it for you—complete with wizards, witches, fabulous beasts, quests, spells, and objects of power.

So find a cozy spot.

Settle in.

And fall under our spell.

Let the magic begin!

Stories grow in different ways. Sometimes they come all in a rush, sometimes in bits and pieces. In the case of this story, I wrote the first few pages (which are now the opening pages of the second section) at a friend's house one night long ago. Then I set it aside until I could figure out what to do with it.

That's one trick you learn as a writer: never throw away your bits and pieces. Sometimes they have magic in them.

WIZARD'S BOY

Bruce Coville

I. The Hungry Heart

"Hey Aaron!" jeered a tall, dirt-smeared boy. "Got any magic to show us today?"

"Careful!" cautioned his companion. "The little wizard might turn you into a toad."

The tall boy made a fake display of terror, holding his hands in front of himself. Then he and his companion collapsed against each other, laughing helplessly.

Keeping his eyes on the under-ripe melons

he had been picking through, Aaron pretended to ignore the boys. But their teasing comments burned inside him. When he finally finished the marketing and returned to the cottage he shared with the wizard Bellenmore, he went to stand in front of the old man and demanded, as he had so many times before, "When will I be ready?"

The wizard glanced up from the lizard he had just taken from its cage. Peering through wire-rimmed spectacles, he scowled at the skinny youngster he had taken in so many years ago. Though he was very fond of Aaron the boy's impatience was beginning to annoy him.

"When?" asked Aaron again.

"I don't have the slightest idea!"

"But Bellenmore—"

"Aaron!" The old man's voice was sharp. "We have gone over this time and again. High Magic is not a toy, not something you play with. Nor is it possible to use until something in you can reach out and touch it. You can't will yourself to be ready for it, any more than you can will yourself to be . . . oh, taller, for heavens' sake. Some people are ready very young. Some are never ready. It's different for everyone."

"You don't want to teach me!" cried Aaron. "You want to keep the power for yourself." A wrenching sob rose in his chest. Rather than release it, he turned and fled the cottage.

Bellenmore dropped the lizard into its carefully decorated cage and went to the door. Silently, he watched the boy leave the clearing where the cottage nestled. Once Aaron had disappeared into the forest, the wizard shook his head sadly, causing his long white hair to ripple over his shoulders. Why were youngsters always so eager for something that was really so very painful?

Well, the boy would get over it. He always did.

He sighed and returned to the lizard, which looked up at him from its favorite rock and said in peeved tones, "I wish you wouldn't drop me like that. I think I sprained my tail."

After Bellenmore apologized, the lizard added, "Don't worry about the boy. If I remember correctly, you were much the same at that age."

The wizard snorted, then pretended that he hadn't heard.

Aaron stumbled blindly through the forest. The air was cold, and a sharp breeze rustled the bloodred leaves. He ran until his breath burned in his lungs. Finally, when he could go no further, he stopped and pressed his forehead against an old oak that had a trunk so thick his arms could barely reach halfway around it.

For a time, he just stood, panting and gasping.

Then he began to walk toward the ravine.

He regretted his sharp words now. He knew they came more from frustration than anything else. He didn't really believe Bellenmore was trying to keep anything to himself. But it was so hard to wait—especially with the boys in the village constantly tormenting him about it.

Aaron sighed. Their jeers and teasing were partly his own fault. When he saw them with their fathers, on the days that he went to town to do the marketing, he was jealous—so jealous he had begun to create stories about his life with the old wizard who had adopted him, wild tales about the great magics Bellenmore was teaching him. Carried away with his own words, he had boasted of how he would soon be a powerful magician himself, while the town boys remained mere apprentices and hired hands.

Naturally, the boys had asked him to show them some magic. Equally naturally, once they found he couldn't, they never let him forget it.

It wouldn't have been quite so painful if he had been able to work even some minor spell to prove he had hope. But no matter how he tried, the magic (both High and Low) refused to come to him. And the truth was, it wasn't that Bellenmore was unwilling to teach him. It was that the teaching did no good; no matter how he tried, Aaron could not touch the currents of magic.

He walked on, his eyes on the ground, so

consumed in his misery he failed to notice the enormous creature that flew overhead.

He did notice, however, the heavy, four-toed footprint that sank deep into the soft ground at the edge of the next stream he came to. He bent to examine it, then wrinkled his brow in concern. It looked like a troll print. But that was ridiculous. There had been no troll sightings in this area for several years now, not since Bellenmore had driven the last of the creatures away.

Aaron glanced around, looking for more footprints. But the leaves that covered the forest floor would not take an impression.

He stood at the edge of the stream, uncertain what to do next. It might be best to go back to the cottage, to report this to Bellenmore right away. But it was too soon; neither his anger nor his chagrin at his own foolishness had cooled enough for him to feel comfortable going back. Besides, it was only one footprint.

Using stepping stones so familiar to him he didn't even need to look at them, Aaron crossed the stream.

The sun was sinking lower in the sky. The breeze seemed to be picking up. An eerie cry in the distance made him shiver, and he thought again about turning back. Bellenmore was quick to forgive. It would be no problem to return now.

But the cry wasn't the sound of a troll—he knew enough about them to know *that.* Besides, he had made up his mind to go to the ravine, and he didn't want to give up on the idea. Walking its edge helped to calm the storms that raged within him.

Bellenmore won't be worried, he told himself. *And I'm no coward, ready to run home because of a weird noise.*

Still, as he walked he found himself glancing around more often than was his habit.

Aaron had another reason to go to the ravine. He had a special spot beside it that he used for practicing. It was where he sat to try and find the quiet place inside himself, the place where Bellenmore claimed the Magic dwelt. Once or twice he thought he actually did catch a touch, for the briefest instant, of some deep power running through him. But it always vanished as soon as he became aware of it. Usually, there was nothing.

He sighed. Maybe Bellenmore was right after all.

The magician was still on Aaron's mind when he reached the ravine. He did love the old man. How could he not? Bellenmore had taken him in after his parents' deaths, reared him like a son. And if his temper was a bit quick, his tongue a trifle sharp, all in all he treated Aaron very well. Aaron knew that many a boy in town would gladly trade places with him, despite all the teasing they gave him.

He stood gazing pensively into the ravine. Far below, at the base of its rocky, brush-cluttered banks, ran a swiftly moving stream. It caught the last of the sun's light now, which made the water look like blood.

The deep silence was shattered by a screech. Aaron spun, aware as he did of the sound of giant wings beating somewhere above him. Suddenly he screamed and threw up his hands to protect himself. A hideous creature was swooping toward him. It was leather-skinned, twice the height of a man, with a wingspread like a house. Its knife-like talons stretched for his throat. Its oddly human face leered with malevolent glee. "Come to me!" it hissed.

"Get back!" cried Aaron, as he stumbled back himself. His foot crossed the edge of the ravine. He lost his balance and went over, bouncing down the steep, rocky slope.

II. The Grangli

Save for the dim light flickering through the windows in the side of the hill, the world seemed made of blackness. Peering through those windows, an intruder would have seen

Bellenmore the Magician pacing back and forth, pulling at his white beard and muttering great imprecations to the walls and furniture.

A green flame crackled on the hearth, holding a cauldron of thick stew at a low boil. Above the fire, on the mantel, a row of gargoyle-festooned mugs winked and smiled hideously, occasionally bursting out in a chorus of bawdy song.

The latch of the door rattled.

Bellenmore sprang for it and snatched the door open. He fell back in surprise as Aaron stumbled in. Twigs and grass clung to the boy's clothing. His face was covered with dark bruises. A trickle of blood had dried behind his right ear.

His eyes were wide, haunted.

Bellenmore seized him by the arms and drew him into the cottage. "Aaron, what happened? Are you all right?"

As the boy gazed at Bellenmore the tumult in his eyes began to quiet. He swallowed twice, then whispered, "The Grangli is flying. I saw it."

Bellenmore dropped his hands. He turned this way and that, as if searching for support, and finally looked back to Aaron. "I'm glad you're safe," he whispered. "Now, let me tend to these wounds, and you can tell me what happened. No, on second thought, you should eat first."

He led the boy to the hearth and settled him

onto a stool. Then he ladled up a plate of the stew and drew a mug of cider from the barrel in the corner. He thrust plate and mug into Aaron's hands. The boy took them gratefully.

As Aaron ate, Bellenmore washed his wounds. Then he worked at healing the boy, both with herbs and potions that were natural, and with spells that would speed their action.

When the healing and the feeding were finished, Bellenmore asked for the story. He paced the floor as the boy spoke of what he had seen, and how only his fall into a narrow crevice had saved him from the monstrous creature.

"The Grangli," muttered Bellenmore in astonishment, once Aaron had finished. "But that can only mean that Dark Anne has returned."

"Brilliant," muttered the lizard.

Far across the wood a wizened woman sat in a cave lit only by the flames that crackled beneath the enormous black cauldron she was stirring. Serpents hissed and crawled about her bare feet. More snakes clung to the stalactites that thrust like giant fangs from the cave's damp ceiling.

Peering into the cauldron's depths, the woman was able to observe the action in Bellenmore's cottage.

A wicked gleam lit her face. "So they know

I'm back," she chuckled. "And they fear what I may do. Well, let them fear, the fools. My power now is greater than Bellenmore would ever dare to dream. And it has just begun to grow." She cackled wildly. "The Grangli flies, and oh, what woe we now shall work on the lands that Bellenmore is bound to protect!"

She snapped her fingers. In an instant the Grangli stood before her, its wings furled in front of it, its head surrounded by the weaving, hissing serpents that hung from the ceiling.

"How did you fare, my pretty one?" cooed the witch. "Did you bring Dark Anne her due?"

The Grangli uttered a strangled cry and produced, from some unknowable place beneath its wings, the torn carcass of a sheep.

Dark Anne was pleased. The animal would provide both dinner and . . . ingredients.

Bellenmore was leaning over an oaken stand, paging through the large, leatherbound book that rested on its surface. He turned the yellowed leaves cautiously, for they were fragile with age.

Aaron stood by the magician's side. He was frustrated because he couldn't do anything to help.

"How could it happen?" he asked, when he

saw Bellenmore pause. "How could she have escaped so quickly?"

The wizard scowled. "I don't know. When last we clashed, and I mastered her so narrowly, I used a spell that should have bound her for lifetimes yet to come. But now the Grangli flies again, and it is obvious Dark Anne has returned. She must have found new power someplace. But where? That's the riddle, Aaron. Her dealings with the dark side have gone on so long already it hardly seems there was anywhere left for her to turn."

The lizard climbed to the top of its cage. Poking its head over the edge it said, "Perhaps she found the Black Stone of Borea." Then it unrolled its tongue, caught a passing fly, and dropped back to the stone on which it had been lounging.

Bellenmore shuddered. "That would have given her the power to escape, all right."

"What's the Black Stone of Borea?" asked Aaron.

Bellenmore twisted his fingers in his beard. "An object of enormous power," he said at last.

"Of course, it's not really a stone," pointed out the lizard.

"Well, it is now," said Bellenmore.

Aaron, who was used to this kind of conversation between the wizard and the lizard, knew very well how long it could go on. Raising his voice, he said, rather sharply, "Please! Just tell me what it is!"

Bellenmore sighed. "The Black Stone of Borea was once the heart of the greatest wizard who ever lived. There is a long and very strange story about his death and how his heart came to be turned to stone—and an even stranger story about how it came to be lodged at the College of Wizards."

"Where it caused all sorts of mischief," said the lizard, its tongue flickering in and out.

"Though the stone is neither good nor evil," continued Bellenmore, "its ability to gather power, to call it forth from unexpected places, to focus it, made it an enormous temptation not only to those of evil intent, but to many of good will who wanted to use its power to twist the world to their vision of goodness."

"Always a dangerous proposition," pointed out the lizard.

Bellenmore nodded. "Finally it was agreed that for the safety of all, the stone should be locked away."

"Where did they put it?" asked Aaron.

Bellenmore shrugged. "No one knows. The spell was designed to send it randomly to one of the places where . . ." He paused, then closed his eyes and moaned.

"What's wrong?" asked Aaron.

Bellenmore passed a hand across his brow. "I

just had a horrible thought. What if when I banished Dark Anne I sent her to the same place as the Black Stone? She would surely have found it—or it her, for it calls to anyone with power. Found it, and freed it, and used it to make her way back. That would explain everything."

His face grim, he said, "If that *is* what happened, then the thing she will be wanting now is revenge—revenge that could take any form, come from any direction, strike at any time. We must double our guard, Aaron, be as watchful as we can. Even then we'll have but small chance of sensing her attack before it is sprung."

"Maybe we should strike first," said Aaron.

Bellenmore turned and peered at him from under thick white brows.

The forest was deep, and dark, and still, the only noise the almost unhearable rustle of softly passing feet. They traveled single file—Bellenmore (the lizard perched on his shoulder), Aaron, and, behind all three, keeping watch at the rear, a minor demon Bellenmore had summoned with a spell of service.

Clouds filled the night sky, blocking the stars and the moon. Aaron kept his hand on Bellenmore's shoulder. The demon walked backwards, the single eye in the back of its head preventing it from stumbling while the stronger eyes in its face scanned the woods behind them for any sign of menace.

The silence was broken by a screech of pain. It came from above them, seeming to fill the sky. The sound put fingers of ice to Aaron's spine.

Even as Bellenmore grabbed the boy and shoved him to the side of the path, a huge shape fell from the blackness, plummeting toward them. Aaron felt the earth tremble when the thing struck the ground.

Bellenmore tapped his staff against a rock and a gentle light grew around them.

Aaron shuddered.

At their feet lay the Grangli. Its massive body was twisted, its semi-human face made more hideous than ever by the pain of its unexpected death.

"This," said the lizard, "does not look good."

"Any ideas on what could have done it?" asked Bellenmore.

The lizard blinked. Then, sounding worried for the first time since Aaron had known it, it asked, very softly, "Malefestra?"

The minor demon hissed.

III. Darkness Gathering

Malefestra! The name burned in Aaron's mind. He had heard it whispered, of course—heard it in old tales, darker tales than he liked to hear. A master of power, a master of wickedness. In the shadow of his presence, their plan to attack Dark Anne seemed like little more than a game.

"I thought he was dead," whispered the boy.

"His kind never dies," replied Bellenmore. "They change. They wait. They go through times of quiet. But they always emerge again sooner or later, stronger than ever, ready to challenge anything that stands between themselves and the power they crave."

He paused, then added, "It would make sense, in a way. If Dark Anne did find the Black Stone and bring it back with her, that might have been enough to stir Malefestra into action. For its power would call to him as surely as it called to her."

"But why would Malefestra kill the Grangli?" asked Aaron. "Wouldn't Dark Anne be on his side?"

"On his side, but never willing to yield to him. I suspect he killed the Grangli to show her his strength, possibly even thinking he might frighten her into submission. I don't believe it will work; she is too fresh from exile, too aware of her own power. Though it could never match his, she won't surrender without a struggle. And he has managed two warnings at once with the killing of the Grangli: one to Dark Anne—and one to us."

* * *

The witch's shriek of rage echoed from the walls of her cave, so startling in its fury that it silenced the hissing of the serpents. Shaking her skinny fists, she cursed the name Malefestra.

"My Grangli is dead!" she screamed. "My beautiful Grangli dead. And it's all his fault. Oh, woe to him now, too. Woe and sorrow and pain. How he shall pay for this!"

In the heat of her anger all caution was lost. She waved her hands over her cauldron and summoned an image of Malefestra. Then through that medium she sent a bolt of power with the intention of destroying the Demon King immediately.

She realized her foolishness at once, but it was too late to call it back. The cauldron shivered. A great gash appeared in its side. Its contents poured out across the floor, thick bubbling liquid splashing about the witch's feet. Hissing in alarm, the snakes slithered away, though several of them were not fast enough to escape being boiled on the spot.

Dark Anne's eyes bloomed large with fear. For a moment she stood like an animal that has just scented a hunter on its trail. Then she snatched something from her shelves, stalked from the cave, and headed into the woods.

* * *

"I can tell you something about this," said the minor demon.

Bellenmore gestured for it to go on.

The creature adjusted its tail, then said, "It has long been rumored in the Otherworld that Malefestra would be on the move again. He has been gathering power and enlisting recruits—trolls, goblins, assorted monsters and creatures—for many months now. Yet many of us fear him, fear that if he is successful, he will make our lives even more miserable than they are already."

Bellenmore nodded. "He probably would. The problem is, how do we stop him?" He tugged at his beard and scowled himself into thought.

Aaron tried to come up with an idea, too. But it was hopeless; he knew too little about all this.

He was still trying to focus his thoughts when a voice screeched, "Bellenmore!"

"As if we didn't have trouble enough already," muttered the lizard.

The call had come from Dark Anne, who was approaching through the forest. Though Aaron felt a surge of terror at the sight of her, the witch raised her hands and growled, "I approach in peace." Her voice was low and gravelly, and Aaron found it somehow both terrifying and exciting.

The witch paused for a moment when she saw the crumpled form of her great flying beast, paused and closed her eyes. Then she made a sign over the broken body and walked on. She stopped a few paces from them and said, "When the time comes we shall be enemies again, Bellenmore—unless you are willing to change your ways and hold your power less tightly. But for now, I bid you join me in confronting an enemy who would destroy us both, who has already struck at the thing I hold most—"

She paused and glanced back at the Grangli. A terrible look of grief twisted her face and a few grains of sand trickled down her withered cheek.

Aaron looked away, embarrassed to witness such sorrow, even in an enemy. But Bellenmore was unmoved. Face stern, voice cold, he said, "I can never work with you."

"That's my boy," said the lizard, in a tone so odd that Aaron really didn't know what he meant.

The old woman sneered. "Don't be a self-righteous idiot. You know how things were the last time Malefestra's power was on the rise—the darkness that covered the land, the innocent blood that was shed. He makes no distinction between your folk and mine, Bellenmore. They suffer equally. Can you stop him by yourself? Will you risk the lives and safety of those who depend on you simply to avoid soiling your hands with the likes of me?" Gesturing to the minor demon, she added, "It's not as if you've been pure in all your dealings until now."

The minor demon hissed at her.

"Wait!" said Bellenmore, as the witch turned to go. When she turned back he nodded and said grimly, "You're right. It is the only way."

Startled, Aaron drew close to Bellenmore. "Can we do that?" he asked in an urgent whisper. "You told me there could be no compromise with her kind."

The wizard frowned. "It is a bad idea, and I fear it. But I see no other way. Should Malefestra conquer, there will be no choices for any of us."

Aaron and Bellenmore had entered the forest seeking Dark Anne. Now she had found them, and they had found a common enemy—or at least found that he had returned.

It was the minor demon who gave them the next step.

"Rumors have Malefestra's headquarters in the Broken Tower," it said. After some discussion, the others agreed that the minor demon should lead them there—primarily, felt Aaron, because Bellenmore and Dark Anne wanted to keep an eye on each other and neither wished to be in front.

Now that they knew their destination, it was decided, somewhat to Aaron's dismay, that they would fly.

The night air chilled the boy as he rose into the sky at Bellenmore's side. He liked flying. But it frightened him, too, mostly because he had no control over his own flight. And though it was Bellenmore who lifted him and guided him, and though he trusted the old magician with all his heart, he still found it terrifying to careen through the air at such speed—and at such a dizzying height—with no control at all.

Night-dark fields streaked by below, as did cottages, huts, the occasional town or village, and here and there a large manor house—all bound in slumber and unaware of the darkness growing among them.

At last the tower rose in view. Aaron shivered at the sight of the monstrous thing. Once tall and splendid, decorated with intricate inlays of ivory and ebony, it had been charred and battered in a clash between chaos and order a millennium ago. The top of the tower had been shattered in that war, and now it rose in jagged points. Brambles grew thick around its base.

"Malefestra must not know of our approach," said Bellenmore as they neared the tower. "We dare not go closer without protection."

Dark Anne hesitated. Then, with a sigh, she drew from her sleeve a black stone half again the size of a man's fist. It gleamed like an ebony fire, and even Aaron could sense the crackle of power that surrounded it.

"The Black Stone of Borea," he whispered in awe. "So you *did* find it."

The hag caressed the stone. "With our combined skills, we can use this to shield ourselves from the enemy's eyes. Neither one alone, but you and I in tandem, Bellenmore, can make this magic work."

Floating high above the ground, the magician reached forward to place his hand on the powerful stone.

For a frightening moment Aaron expected betrayal. But he saw Bellenmore smile, ever so slightly, as a thrill of power raced through him. Then the wizard's brow darkened in concentration as Dark Anne began to chant. Working together, the two magicmakers threw a shield about the little group.

Moments later, they landed on the narrow stone ledge that was all that remained of the tower's highest floor. Around them rose the remains of the wall. They made Aaron think of giant teeth.

"Now what?" he whispered.

"We go down," replied the minor demon. "Deep into the tower to face Malefestra. There is no other way."

IV. The Prisoner

For a moment Aaron wondered why the demon was so intent. But Bellenmore and Dark Anne nodded their agreement, and together the mortal three followed their guide onto a crumbling stair that led them in a slow, spiral descent into the tower.

Darkness seemed to swallow them. The walls were dank, yet Aaron pressed against them, for fear of falling off the stair and plummeting into a void for which he could see no bottom. As they continued downward the air began to change, growing cold and foul, and heavy in the lungs. Aaron wanted desperately to cough, but feared he would give them away if he did. So he held it in, though the urge grew until it was like a torment.

Once something fluttered close to him, the sound of wings in the darkness so startling that he nearly leapt away from them. He only saved himself from hurtling into the darkness by an enormous effort of will.

At last Bellenmore whispered, "The floor is solid here. We can stop for a moment."

"A bit of light would be safe," said the demon.

Bellenmore's staff began to glow. In the dim light he examined the walls, then nodded in satisfaction. "I have studied this tower in my books. We are near the room where Malefestra would most likely seat himself, on a throne that once held kings."

"What are you going to do when we get to that room?" asked Aaron.

Bellenmore glanced at Dark Anne, but directed his answer to Aaron. "This will be a battle of power. Skills, some. But mostly raw power. And every bit we have on our side will be important. We will spend it, spend it all. That is the only reason you are here, Aaron, for I do not like to put you in harm's way like this. You are to stay out of the throne room, away from the battle. If we lose, then flee. But if we win, and still live, then I expect we will need you to minister to us, for a victory here will come only at great cost. If we win, but do not survive—well, at least there will be someone to tell the story."

Despite his terror, Aaron ached with shame that he had nothing more to contribute to the battle, no power, no magic to throw against their enemy.

Bellenmore turned to Dark Anne. "Are you ready?"

Her answer came in a scratchy whisper. "As ready as you, wizard. But we need to take him by surprise. No more chatter. Let us move on."

Another flight of steps led them to a set of doors three times Aaron's height. They were made of bronze and worked with evil figurings. Witch and wizard each took one of the handles, then chanted spells to loose all locks.

With a nod to one another, they threw wide the doors and burst through to meet Malefestra.

The room was huge and high, and empty.

The minor demon broke into laughter. Then, as Aaron watched in horror, it began to change, to throb and grow until it was revealed at last in its own true shape: The Demon King, Malefestra.

Bellenmore and Dark Anne shouted in rage, but were held by a band of shimmering gray light that wrapped around them. As they struggled against it, Malefestra stepped into the throne room. He towered over them. Huge, batlike wings sprouted from his powerfully muscled shoulders. His legs were like flaming tree trunks, his chest as broad as the hearth in Bellenmore's cottage. But of his face Aaron saw nothing, for resting on the Demon King's shoulders was a cloud of smoke, from which licked an occasional tongue of fire.

From that smoke came a deep, oily voice that was rich with satisfaction. "Oh, my fine sheep. How easily you were led to the slaughter!"

At that moment, Bellenmore and Dark Anne burst free of the gray light. They flung their strongest magics at the Demon King. But surprise they had none, and he was well armored against their attack. Light and power sizzled and struck around him, but could not seem to touch him.

Then he made a gesture and green smoke

began to curl about the witch and the magician. Dark Anne cried out in pain and rage. The Black Stone of Borea fell from her hand and began to roll across the floor.

Aaron dove for it, but with a flick of his finger, Malefestra unleased a force that sent the boy crashing back against the wall.

An enormous sphere of liquid scarlet appeared and wrapped itself around Bellenmore and Dark Anne. The sphere shimmered evilly for a moment, then began to shrink. It grew smaller and smaller, until finally it disappeared, taking Dark Anne, Bellenmore, and the lizard with it.

Alone with Malefestra, Aaron sprang at the Demon King, fury in his eyes. "Bring them back!" he screamed. "Bring them back!"

He never touched the enemy. The Demon King made a sign with his fingers, and Aaron bounced away harmlessly.

"Idiot child," murmured the monster. "Did you expect to lay hands on me? Surely your master has taught you better than that. Or do I overestimate the wisdom of Bellenmore?"

Aaron burned with shame. But he said nothing. From the corner of his eye he judged the distance to the Black Stone.

Malefestra laughed, and the sound boomed around Aaron, seeming to press him to the floor. Then the Demon King snapped his fingers and the stone leaped to his hand.

"Idiot child," he repeated.

He gestured once more and a cage began to form out of the air surrounding Aaron. Iron bars rose and curved above his head, meeting in a ring at the top. Beneath his feet a plate of cold metal grew to form a floor.

At another signal from Malefestra the cage floated slowly into the air, rising until the ring at the top slipped over a great hook embedded in the rock of the ceiling, some thirty feet above the floor.

Days dragged by, but with no way to measure them Aaron lost track of the time. Small amounts of food and water appeared in his cage every once in a while—enough to keep him alive, but never enough to satisfy his young body. He grew thin, while watching the guests of his captor feast.

And guests there were many, for the stream of visitors through the throne room seemed endless. Aaron was fascinated, and frightened, by the parade of evil things that came to pay homage to the master risen among them. Towering trolls and squat, snout-faced goblins passed below him, along with other things for which he had no name—creeping, crawling things. Most of them snorted with amusement when they noticed the boy in his cage, dangling from the stone ceiling.

Each visitor brought some gift to Malefestra, and the pile of spoils on his left-hand side grew higher by the day. But on his right side there was nothing save a seemingly empty pedestal. Aaron knew that seeming to be false. He had watched the Demon King render the Black Stone invisible and then place it lovingly on the pedestal. Ever and again, when he was alone, the Demon King would reach out to stroke the stone.

When Aaron slept (which could have been day or night, he had no way of telling) he had strange dreams. Sometimes he heard Bellenmore and Dark Anne calling out for help. Other times he would see the stone rise from its pedestal and thunder toward him. Then he would wake with cold sweat running down his face, and his body trembling.

He grew fascinated, obsessed with the stone. Sometimes he actually thought it was calling to him. His hands ached to hold it and he would grip the bars of his cage until his knuckles went white. He would shake it in his fury, and weep for Bellenmore. But there was nothing he could do. He had no power.

V. The Deepest Current

A time came when Malefestra called his servants to a feast. Goblins, demons, ogres, trolls, certain wicked dwarfs, a small dragon, and a handful of ghouls gathered in the Broken Tower for a celebration that quickly fell into a drunken brawl. The trolls were beating the floor, and each other, with their clubs. Goblins leapt about on the tables, flinging food in all directions. Several ogres decided they would prefer some fresh dwarf to the food being served. The dwarves thought this was a bad idea. The noise, and the smell, were appalling.

The Demon King watched in amusement for a time. Then, as if bored with the whole affair, he left on some private business.

In the Broken Tower the revellers revelled on. The party reached new heights of hilarity as mock battles were staged across the throne room floor. Tables and chairs were shattered. Soon clubs appeared, then rocks and spears. It was not long before the battles were no longer mock, but deadly serious, as short tempers, fueled by wine and ale, flared high.

One misplaced club, flying far from its mark, struck the hook from which Aaron's cage was suspended.

The boy held his breath. The hook, set in the stone ceiling, swung gently back and forth with the movement of the cave. And each time it swung, it pulled its way just a tiny bit farther out of the ceiling.

Aaron gripped the bars and waited without

moving. Beneath him the brawl raged on, surging around the room, until at last all had fallen, either from drink or from well-placed clubs and fists.

Aaron leaned to his right. The cage swung. The hook moved.

He shifted his weight and the cage swung back.

He began to rock with a gentle rhythm. Slowly, the hook began to worm its way free.

If only he could get it out before Malefestra returned!

Hours passed, and finally the cage did come loose. Aaron had a moment of terror as it plummeted to the floor. His fall was broken by the body of a sleeping troll, who would now sleep even longer.

The impact of the fall jarred the door loose.

Aaron crept out of the cage and looked about cautiously. All were sleeping. Halfway across the room stood Malefestra's throne. Beside it, invisible, was the Black Stone of Borea.

Aaron picked his way across the room, stepping carefully over outflung arms and twitching legs, avoiding for his life the various demon tails that crossed his path. Several times he slipped in puddles of spilled ale, once actually landing on the flabby green stomach of a fur-clad ogre. It opened its enormous single eye, belched in disgust, and fell back into slumber.

The closer he drew to the throne, and the stone, the greater was Aaron's terror. Each instant he feared that Malefestra would return.

Heart pounding, he climbed the throne. When he was finally able to reach out and touch the unseen stone, he almost fainted at the flood of power that coursed through his body.

Dizzy with strength, with uncertainty, he snatched the stone and hurried back to his cage. Climbing inside, he tucked the stone into his shirt, where it rested against his skin, comforting and strengthening him.

He needed time to think.

He had little of it, for not more than ten minutes later Malefestra returned. Yet his rage at seeing the shambles of the feast was not as the boy had expected. Knowing his servants, the Demon King had known what to expect when they convened, and it was a simple matter for him to use his power to set the room right.

He seemed more perturbed over the fall of Aaron's cage.

Trying to control his trembling, Aaron lay as though he had been knocked senseless by the fall. Without leaving his throne, Malefestra resealed the cage door and caused the whole thing to float back to the ceiling, along with the hook which had held it.

Not until he reached out to touch the Black

Stone of Borea was the wrath of the Demon King aroused.

"Where is it?" he roared. Behind the rage, his voice held a scarcely detectable note of panic. But it was the power of his anger that roused every creature in the room. A frightened murmur rippled through the hall as the trolls, goblins, and ogres began stumbling nervously to their feet.

Malefestra cried out in rage once more. Now all were attentive, alert, and trembling.

But Malefestra stopped his ranting and seemed to grow calm. He spread his enormous arms and stood trembling with the effort of detection. Slowly, he turned toward Aaron's cage. A prickle of fear went sliding down the boy's spine. He grabbed the Black Stone, clutching it to his stomach.

Mistake. The moment his hands touched the stone, Malefestra knew.

"*You* have it!" he cried. And for the second time that night Aaron's cage crashed to the floor. With no troll to cushion its landing this time, the cage struck with a bone-splintering crash. The cage itself shattered. Aaron was thrown free, and the Black Stone fell from his grasp. Invisible, it rolled across the floor.

"Seize it!" cried Malefestra. At the same moment he gestured for it to come to him.

But Aaron was quicker this time. Almost before the stone had fallen from his hands he was after it. Ignoring his pain, he scrambled across the floor, managing to find and hold it.

The others leapt upon him, and for a moment he felt as if he would be crushed. The moment passed in an explosion of screaming and screeching. The assorted monsters were thrown from Aaron's back as though by some gigantic hand.

Aaron stood. But this was no longer Aaron, apprentice to a master. Rather it was an Aaron whose power and strength had been quickened by the Black Stone of Borea, an Aaron who had finally tapped the currents of magic that lay deep within him, and found that the power he had ached so long to feel was now surging through him, joining with the power of the stone. Somehow, without knowing how, he knew how to use the stone. And so he stood and held it high above his head, trembling with its strength.

Power crackled through the air. Shrieking, the minions of Malefestra fell to the floor and covered their heads. The Dark Lord himself was not so easily broken. Throwing up a shield, he protected himself from the power Aaron had unleashed.

"Put it down, child," he said smoothly, the words drifting from the smoke that curled where his head should be. "Put it down, and you may be allowed to live when this is over."

But the power that had woken in Aaron was still growing. Filled with pride, he threw back his head and laughed.

His second mistake. For now the Demon King was angered indeed. Aaron's laughter had fueled Malefestra's hate, and his strength. The shield about him shattered and the power that had been Aaron's swirled madly about the room to rush back at the boy.

"No!" cried Aaron. He held the stone before him. The power struck, and was absorbed by the stone. Instantly it grew hot and began to burn against his flesh.

Now it was Aaron's turn to be frightened. Bolt after bolt of power came crashing toward him. Though he used the stone to capture every one, it grew hotter and hotter with each bolt of power it absorbed. Soon the boy felt his flesh begin to sear. When the sickening smell of burning skin hit his nostrils he nearly vomited in terror.

Yet he dared not let the stone go; to drop it would mean death.

"Surrender!" roared Malefestra, and again the air was slashed with power. "Surrender!"

Aaron fell to his knees. But still he would not let go of the stone, which was glowing now with the power it had absorbed. It seemed to burn him to the very bone.

"Surrender!" cried Malefestra again.

"Never!" whispered Aaron, his throat so tight the sound could barely pass. "Never."

And then the stone erupted. All the power it had taken in burst free, and a bolt of enormous energy shot across the room. The stone itself exploded into a thousand pieces. From somewhere far away Aaron heard a cry of anguished pain. Then there was silence.

Malefestra lay unmoving on the floor.

Unable to move, unable to speak, Aaron knelt and stared at his hands, oblivious to the chaos erupting around him.

The legions of Malefestra, which had quivered against the walls during the battle, now began to rouse themselves. Their babble grew louder, until at last it penetrated Aaron's daze.

Without looking up, he waved his hand and cried, "Begone!"

The forces of darkness fled squalling into the night, scattering to their separate holes and hiding places in the darkness of the earth.

And still the boy knelt and stared at his hands, on which no burns could be seen, but which throbbed with a pain so fierce it felt as if he were holding them in a fire, and pulsed with a strength that made him weak to think of it.

At last his lips parted. "Bellenmore," he whispered. "Help me."

"Alas, you'll have to help yourself, my boy," said a faint voice behind him.

Aaron turned, and saw the magician, who had been called back by the power of his words. (By *my* power, Aaron realized in astonishment.)

Then he realized that something was wrong. Though he could see Bellenmore, the wizard's form was hazy, shimmering. He reached toward him, and his hand went through the image.

The wizard shook his head sadly. "There's always a price, Aaron. Always a price. You were right—I should not have joined forces with the dark side, even in the cause of good. I cannot come back, Aaron, at least not yet. Even to speak to you like this is painful, and difficult. I will contact you when I can. I will watch as I am able. But you must fend for yourself now. You've found your power. It's time to go back to the cottage, and learn how to use it."

His form wavered and he disappeared from view, even as Aaron fell to his knees moaning, "Come back, come back!"

When he finally lifted his head, he noticed the lizard coiled on the floor in front of him.

"I didn't agree to the deal with Dark Anne," it said. "I got to come back. Come on. Let's go home."

Picking up the lizard, Aaron made his way from the tower.

* * *

Aaron sat on the edge of the ravine and watched the sun rise. It had been two weeks since the battle in the Broken Tower, and though his hands still throbbed with pain now and then, he had mostly recovered.

And the land—the land that Bellenmore was sworn to protect—was peaceful. The light of the rising sun lay in golden pools among the leaves, burnished acorns scattered like jewels in their midst. A soft breeze washed across him, carrying news from all across the earth.

He enjoyed the quiet. And he was learning to live with the newness that was in him, the thing that had been struggling to be born all these months and had been finally unleashed by need and terror in the tower of the Demon King.

Aaron turned his gaze back to the ancient book of power that lay in his lap.

The lizard coiled on his shoulder whispered an explanation of what the words meant.

Deep within him, Aaron felt the surge and the ebb of a power he still did not understand, but that he knew would mark the days of his life forever after.

He turned the page, and continued to study.

I have often visited Jane Yolen at her home, which is known as Phoenix Farm. I think it is a good name for a place where magic happens. This story is not about Jane, or her home. But now you know where the title came from!

PHOENIX FARM

Jane Yolen

We moved into Grandma's farm right after our apartment house burned down along with most of the neighborhood. It was not a good California summer, dry as popcorn and twice as salty, what with all the sweat running down our faces.

I didn't mind so much—the fire, I mean. I had hated that apartment, with its pockmarked walls and the gang names scribbled on the stoop. Under my bedroom window someone had painted the words "Some day, sugar, you gonna find no one in this world gonna give you sweet." The grammar bothered me more than what it said.

Mama cried, though. About the photos, mostly. And about all her shoes burned up. She has real tiny feet and her one vanity is shoes. She can buy the model stuff for really cheap. But then she cries about everything these days. It's been that way ever since Daddy died.

Ran off. That's what Nicky says. *A week before the fire. Couldn't take it. The recession and all. No job. No hope.*

Mama says it won't be forever, but I say he died. I can deal with it that way.

And besides, we don't want him back.

So we got ready to head for Grandma's farm up in the valley with only the clothes we'd been wearing; our cat, Tambourine; and Mama's track medals all fused together. She found them when the fire fighters let us go back upstairs to sort through things. Nicky grabbed a souvenir, too. His old basketball. It was flat and blackened, like a pancake someone left on the stove too long.

I looked around and there was nothing I wanted to take. Nothing. All that I cared about had made it through the fire: Mama, Nicky, and Tam. It was as if we could start afresh and all the rest of it had been burned away. But as we were going down the stairs—the iron stairs, not the wooden ones inside, which were all gone—I saw the most surprising thing. On the thirteenth step up from the bottom, tucked against the riser, was a nest. It was unburned, unmarked, the straw that held it the rubbed-off gold of a wheat field. A piece of red string ran through it, almost as if it had been woven on a loom. In the nest was a single egg.

It didn't look like any egg I'd ever seen before, not dull white or tan like the eggs from the store. Not even a light blue like the robin's egg I'd found the one summer we'd spent with Grandma at the farm. This was a shiny, shimmery gray-green egg with a red vein—like the red thread—cutting it in half.

"Look!" I called out. But Mama and Nicky were already in the car, waiting. So without thinking it all the way through—like what was I going to do with an egg, and what about the egg's mother, and what if it broke in the car or, worse, hatched—I picked it up and stuck it in the pocket of my jacket. Then, on second thought, I took off the jacket and made a kind of nest of it, and carefully carried the egg and my jacket down the rest of the stairs.

When I got into the car, it was the very first time I had ever ridden in the back all alone without complaining. And all the way to the farm, I kept the jacket-nest and its egg in my lap. All the way.

Grandma welcomed us, saying: "I'm not surprised. Didn't I tell you?" Meaning that Daddy wasn't with us. She and Mama didn't fight over it, which was a surprise on its own. Neighbors of hers had collected clothes for us. It made us feel like refugees, which is an awkward feeling that makes you prickly and cranky most of the time. At least that's how I felt until I found the green sweater that exactly matches my eyes and Nicky found a Grateful Dead T-shirt. There were no shoes Mama's size. And no jobs nearby, either.

I stashed the egg in its jacket-nest on the dresser Mama and I shared. Nicky, being the only boy, got his own room. Mama never said a word about the egg. It was like she didn't even see it. I worried what she'd say if it began to smell.

But the days went by and the egg never did begin to stink. We got settled into our new school. I only thought about Daddy every *other* day. And I found a best friend right away. Nicky had girls calling him after dinner for the first time. So we were okay.

Mama wasn't happy, though. She and Grandma didn't exactly quarrel, but they didn't exactly get along, either. Being thankful to someone doesn't make you like them. And since Mama couldn't find a job, they were together all day long.

Then one evening my new best friend Ann

Marie was over. We were doing homework together up in my room. It was one of those coolish evenings and the windows were closed, but it was still pretty bright outside, considering.

Ann Marie suddenly said, "Look! Your egg is cracking open."

I looked up and she was right. We hadn't noticed anything before, because the crack had run along the red line. When I put my finger on the crack, it seemed to pulse.

"Feel that!" I said.

Ann Marie touched it, then jerked back as if she had been burned. "I'm going home now," she said.

"But Ann Marie, aren't you the one who dragged me to see all those horror movies and—"

"Movies aren't real," she said. She grabbed up her books and ran from the room.

I didn't even say good-bye. The egg had all my attention, for the gray-green shell seemed to be taking little breaths, pulsing in and out, in and out, like a tiny brittle ocean. Then the crack widened, and as if there was a lamp inside, light poured out.

Nicky came in then, looking for some change on the dresser.

"Neat!" he said when he saw the light. "Do you know what kind of bird it's going to be? Did you look it up in Dad—" And then he

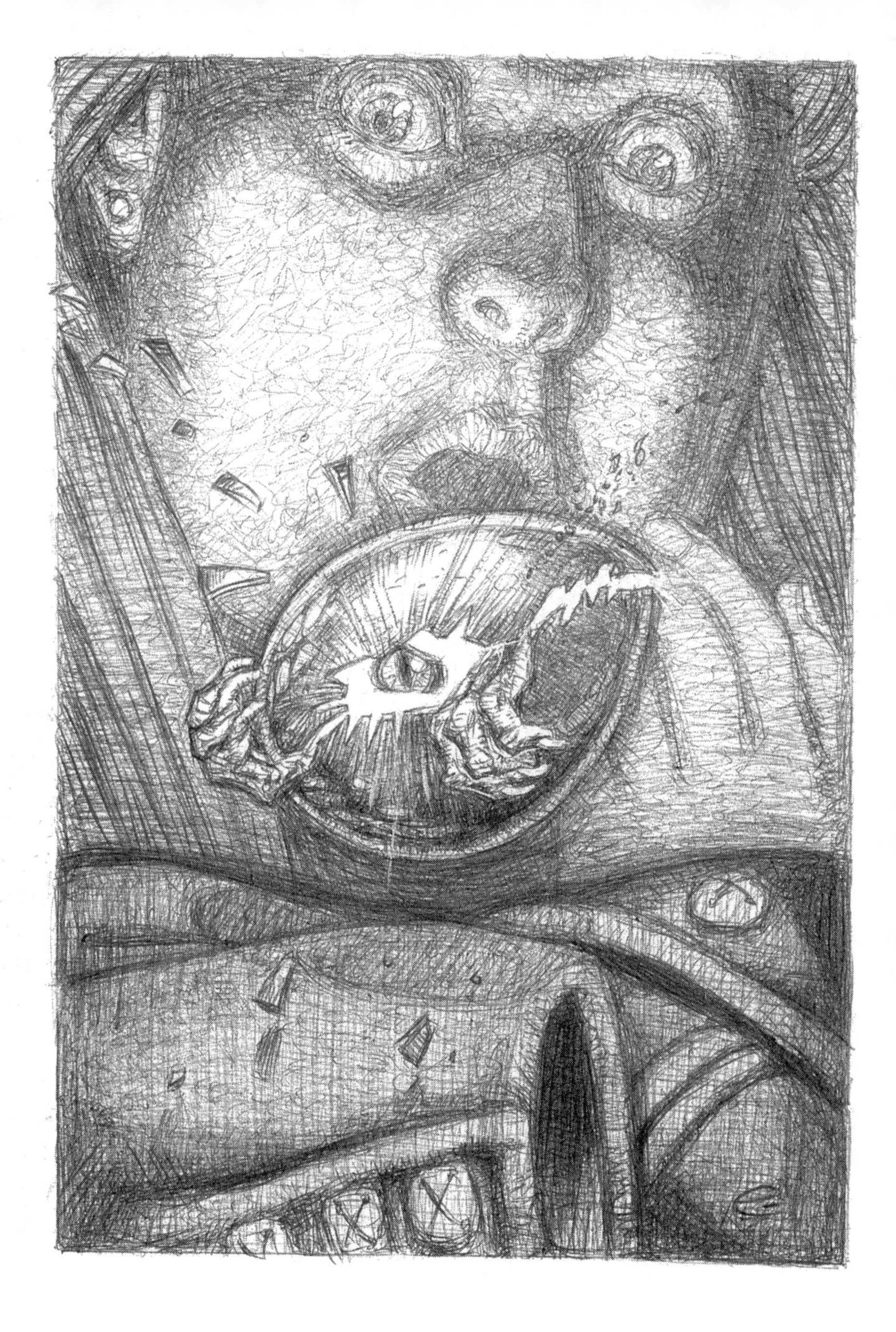

stopped because all of Daddy's books had been burned up. Besides, we didn't mention him anymore. And since we hadn't heard from him at all, it was like he really *was* dead.

"No," I said. "And I don't think it's any *ordinary* bird that you would find in an *ordinary* book."

"A lizard, you think?"

Never taking my eyes off the egg, I shook my head. How stupid could he be? With that light coming out? A dragon, maybe. Then the phone rang downstairs and he ran out of the room, expecting, I guess, that it would be Courtney or Brittany or another of his girlfriends named after spaniels. Talking to them was more important to him than my egg.

But I continued to watch. I was the only one watching when it hatched. How such a large bird got into such a small egg, I'll never know. But that's magic for you. It rose slowly out of the egg, pushing the top part of the shell with its golden head. The beak was golden, too, and curved like one of those Arabian swords. The eyes were hooded and dark, without a center, so that when it stared at me, I felt drawn in.

The bird gave a sudden kind of shudder and humped itself further out of the egg, and its wings were blue and scarlet and gold, all shimmery like some seashells when they're wet. It shook out its wings and they were wide enough to touch from one side of the dresser to the other, the individual feathers throwing off sparkles of light.

Another shudder, and the bird stood free of the egg entirely, though a piece of shell still clung to the tip of one wing. I reached over and freed it, and it seared my fingers—the touch of the feather, not the shell. The bird's scarlet body and scaley golden feet pulsed with some kind of heat.

"What *are* you?" I whispered, then stuck my burned fingers in my mouth to soothe them.

If the bird could answer me, it didn't; it just pumped its wings, which seemed to grow wider with each beat. The wind from them was a Santa Ana, hot and heavy and thick.

I ran to the window and flung it wide, holding the curtain aside.

The bird didn't seem to notice my effort, but still it flew unerringly outside. I saw it land once on a fencepost, a second time on the roof of Grandma's barn. Then it headed straight toward the city, the setting sun making a fire in its feathers.

When I couldn't see it anymore, I turned around. The room smelled odd—like the ashes of the fire, but like something else, too. Cinnamon, maybe. Or cloves.

I heard the doorbell. It rang once, then a second time. Grandma and Mama were off visiting a neighbor. Nicky was still on the phone. I ran down the stairs and flung the door wide open.

Daddy was standing there, a new beard on his face and a great big Madame Alexander doll box in his arms.

"I got a job, baby. In Phoenix. And a house rented. With a real backyard. I didn't know about the fire, I didn't know where you all had gone. My letters came back and the phone didn't connect and . . ."

"Daddy!" I shouted, and he dropped the box to scoop me up against his chest. As I snuggled my face against his neck, I smelled that same smell: ashes and cinnamon, maybe cloves. Where my burned fingers tangled in his hair they hurt horribly. Grandma would be furious. Nicky and Mama might be, too. But I didn't care. There's dead. And there's not.

Sometimes it's better to rise up out of the ashes, singing.

If Jason had read his fairy tales, he would have known that you should be nice to old ladies, whether you meet them in an enchanted forest—or in the 7-Eleven!

HORSING AROUND

Lawrence Watt-Evans

It isn't every day you meet a witch at the 7-Eleven. Jason thought it was a gag—right up until she tried to turn him into a horse.

He and Gus had been arguing about what seventh grade was going to be like, and whether the teachers were all geeks the way Gus's older sister Susannah said they were. They had been so busy arguing, in fact, that Jason had pushed through the door of the 7-Eleven without looking where he was going and almost walked right into the witch.

She was standing at the magazine rack by the door, browsing through stuff like *Cosmopolitan* and *Vogue.* She was dressed in a ratty floor-length black gown that would need cleaning to qualify as filthy. Her greasy, waist-length black hair was unbelievably tangled, and her pointed black hat was so tall that she'd have to duck to get through the door. Her nose was spectacularly long and crooked.

"Hey," Jason said when he'd stopped just short of her and gotten a good look, "isn't it a little early for Halloween?"

"Ha-ha," she said, looking him in the eye. She turned back to the magazines.

Ordinarily Jason would have dropped it right there, but Gus said, "Wow, Jase, killer dialogue you've got there."

That was a challenge.

"So, guess you read those magazines for beauty tips?" Jason said. "*Witch* ones?"

The witch stared at him silently.

Jason desperately wanted to come up with something really clever, but with those dark eyes looking right at him, his brain seemed to stop working. "Hey, Horseface," he began, planning a remark about using a currycomb instead of a hairbrush.

He couldn't think how to finish it, and for a moment he and the witch just stared at each other.

"If anyone around here is behaving like part of a horse's anatomy," the witch said, "I'd say it's you."

Jason swallowed and tried to think of a comeback.

"Seems to me you might as well look the part," the witch said. She raised her hands and began mumbling something that sounded so weird it made the hairs on the back of Jason's neck stand up.

Before she could finish, Gus rammed into her side in a sudden body check. "Oops, slipped," he said as she stumbled against the magazine rack.

The man behind the counter looked up from the six-pack of soda and bag of corn chips he'd been ringing up. "Hey, you boys get out of here and stop bothering my customers!"

"Come on," Gus said, pulling at Jason's sleeve.

Jason came, stumbling back out through the door. He felt really strange.

"I think she tried to put a spell on me," he said once they were outside in the parking lot, only realizing how stupid it sounded after the words were out.

"Is that what she was doing?" Gus said, and punched Jason on the arm. "I thought she was getting ready for one of those kung fu moves or something. That's why I bumped her."

"Yeah—well, thanks," Jason said. His legs felt peculiar, full of twinges and twitches, a little like they did sometimes after a really long run. And his shoes were pinching.

"You okay, Jase?" Gus asked.

"No," Jason said. He kicked off his shoes; now his pants seemed too tight around the ankles.

"Maybe you better sit down," Gus suggested. He looked around for somewhere to sit.

Jason shook his head as he leaned on the hood of a pickup. His legs didn't want to bend right; sitting down was not what he needed. In fact, without knowing why, he was standing on his toes.

His legs felt as if they were splitting right down the middle. He looked down at his stocking feet and almost screamed.

They were changing shape. And they *were* splitting down the middle, the front and back separating.

His socks tore a moment later; then the legs of his jeans began to split.

"Wow," Gus said, staring. "Like the Incredible Hulk on TV!"

"She *did* cast a spell!" Jason shouted. He looked at his toes merging into hooves and said, "I'm turning into a horse!"

"Your face is still okay," Gus said. He was trying to stay calm, but Jason could see from his expression how scared he was.

And if Gus was scared just *watching* . . .

Then Gus's words registered, and Jason realized that in fact he didn't feel any changes in his face, or, for that matter, anywhere above his waist.

Below his waist, though, was another matter. He unbuckled his belt before the squeezing turned into actual pain.

His jeans were ruined; both legs were split. The side seams were gone all the way to the waistband. He straightened up and looked down.

He couldn't even see his back legs from this angle. He turned and looked over his shoulder.

There he was, covered with reddish brown hair; he twitched something that itched, a part of him that hadn't been there a moment before, and saw a newly acquired dark brown tail, just the color of his hair, flick up.

"I'm turning into a *horse!*" Jason shouted.

"I don't think so," Gus said. "I think you've stopped. Maybe I interrupted her before she finished the spell."

"So I'm going to stay *half* a horse?" Somehow, Jason didn't find this significantly better.

"You're a whaddayacallit, Jase—a centaur. That's not so bad. I mean, at least you can still talk and everything."

Suddenly Jason realized he was standing in the parking lot with no pants on, just the ragged remains of a pair of jeans dangling from his waist.

"Gus, what am I going to *do?*" Jason looked around for someplace to hide, but there wasn't anywhere a centaur would fit.

Gus considered the situation, and Jason watched him hopefully. Gus grimaced in concentration; then at last he spoke.

"I don't know, Jase."

"Fat lot of help *you* are!" Jason snapped. He looked around, almost panicking. "I better apologize to her—I mean, I guess I said some rotten stuff. I don't know what got into me. Maybe she'll turn me back."

"Good idea."

They walked to the door of the 7-Eleven, and Gus pulled it open. Jason started to enter the store and discovered he had to duck slightly to clear the doorframe.

"Hey," the clerk shouted, "you can't bring a horse in here!"

"I'm *not* a horse!" Jason shouted back. "I'm a . . . a centaur!"

The clerk glared, chewing his lip, then called, "Well, you still can't come in here! You aren't decent! And you're barefoot!" He pointed to a sign that read: NO SHIRT, NO SHOES, NO SERVICE.

"But—" Jason began.

"Out!" the clerk shouted.

Jason reluctantly backed out.

"Don't worry, Jase, I'll find her," Gus said. He stepped inside, leaving Jason to stand in the parking lot, worrying and horribly aware of people staring at him.

By the time Gus reappeared, Jason had collected a small crowd. None of them dared come too close, and no one spoke to him, but they all stared, and he could hear them talking among themselves.

"It's some kind of trick," someone said as he watched Jason.

"Like the fake unicorn in the circus," a woman agreed.

Jason didn't know what to say to that, so he didn't say anything. He just shuffled his hooves uneasily until Gus emerged and said, "She's not there, Jase."

"Where'd she *go*, then? She didn't come out this way!"

Gus shrugged. "For all I know, she vanished in a puff of smoke. She's not in there, though. I went up and down every single aisle."

"*Now* what do I do?" Jason wailed.

"I dunno," Gus said.

"Who's going to turn me back?"

Gus shrugged again. "Maybe it'll wear off."

Jason snatched at that idea. "Yeah, I bet it will. I bet I'll wake up tomorrow the same as ever. I'll probably turn back into a pumpkin at midnight, like in *Cinderella.*"

"So what're you going to do for today, then?" Gus asked, with a glance at the crowd.

Jason said, "I'd better get home." He tried to pick up his shoes, but discovered he couldn't reach them: even with his forelegs bent, his hands didn't come close to the ground.

Gus saw the problem and handed Jason the sneakers. Jason took them without a word, tied the shoes together by the laces, and hung them around his neck—though he wasn't quite sure what use his shoes were ever going to be to him again if the spell *didn't* wear off.

He began walking dejectedly toward home. The crowd started to follow, but Jason turned and shouted, "Go away! Show's over!"

For a moment no one moved; then, muttering, they dispersed, slowly and reluctantly.

"Jase, there could be possibilities in this centaur stuff," Gus said.

"Shut up," Jason answered. He was not interested, not unless Gus had some way to turn him back to normal.

"No, *really*. I bet you can run like anything, now! And you could give people rides. . . ."

"I'm not even sure how I'm *walking,*" Jason pointed out. "If I stop and think about it, I'll probably trip over my own feet. I'm not about to try running."

"Oh, but—"

"Just shut up, okay, Gus?"

Jason walked on in morose silence, listening to the unfamiliar clop of his hooves on the sidewalk. The sidewalk was awfully far away, too. He hadn't really noticed the change while it was happening, but ever since he had almost hit his head on that doorway, he had known that he was considerably taller now. Judging himself against Gus, he estimated that he was now a good six and a half feet tall, maybe more.

Which might have been pretty cool, if the bottom half hadn't been horse—and naked.

"I can't believe I'm walking down the street without my pants," he said. "It's like one of those awful dreams where you go to school in your pajamas."

"I bet," Gus agreed.

Jason suddenly perked up. "Hey, that's it," he said. "This is all a bad dream, right? I'm just dreaming?" He pinched his arm, the way people did in books and movies.

It hurt. And nothing changed.

"I don't think it's a dream, Jase," Gus said. "I mean, if it is, I'm having it, too."

"I guess it isn't," Jason said.

At last they reached Jason's house, and together the two walked up the driveway to the kitchen door.

The roof of the carport seemed uncomfortably close overhead, Jason thought. He knew it hadn't moved; he was just taller.

He opened the door and stepped in—and stepped in the rest of the way; it took a moment to get all four feet inside. His hooves thumped loudly on the linoleum.

"Wow, Jase," Gus said. "What's your mother gonna say?"

"I don't know," Jason said unhappily.

"Is that you, Jason?" his mother's voice called from the living room.

Jason looked at Gus. Gus shrugged.

"Jason?" his mother called. He heard her footsteps, and for a moment he wanted to hide—but she would have to find out sooner or later. He couldn't hide forever.

And besides, the whole thing still didn't seem completely real. Maybe when his mother looked at him he'd be normal again, and it would all be over.

Then she stepped into the kitchen and saw him.

Jason had heard and read about such things for years, but he had never actually seen anybody faint before.

Centaurs don't kneel well, Jason discovered, and they aren't very good at sitting, either; he was more comfortable standing than in any other position. That wasn't really a big surprise, since he knew horses sleep standing up, but it meant that he towered over his mother when Gus brought her around.

She almost fainted again.

At last she recovered enough to order, "Out of my kitchen!"

"But, Mom . . . !"

"Out!"

Reluctantly, Jason backed out—there wasn't enough room for him to turn around without knocking something over. He hit the back of his head on the doorframe and stood in the carport rubbing it as Gus stepped out of the house with Jason's mother.

"Hi, Mom," Jason said.

"Jason, what *happened?*" she demanded.

"Well, there was a witch at the 7-Eleven. . . ."

His mother listened silently to the whole story, then said, "If you weren't standing there in front of me I wouldn't believe a word of it. Witches and centaurs? You've ruined your jeans. And I've told you to be polite to strangers!"

"I know," Jason said unhappily.

"And you can't come in the house like that."

Jason remembered how tight a fit it had been in the kitchen. "I guess not," he agreed. "But where'll I sleep? What'll I eat?"

His mother didn't have a quick answer to that.

Eventually, however, they cleared out the

backyard shed for him and put in a layer of blankets so that he could lie down if he wanted.

As for food, his mother brought it out to him. He had been afraid he might have to eat grass, but he found that he could eat most ordinary foods with no problem—with one exception.

He couldn't eat meat.

It still tasted fine, but when it reached his stomach he got horrible cramps. His digestion wasn't quite human anymore, and the horse part was herbivorous.

He'd never thought about being a vegetarian, but lots of people managed it. He supposed he could live with it—but he hoped it wasn't permanent.

By the time his father got home Jason was fairly well settled in his shed, and the situation was almost beginning to seem normal, though he missed watching TV and playing video games.

His father didn't see it as normal at all.

He didn't faint; instead, he stopped dead in his tracks and stared.

Jason told the story again. It took longer for his father to accept it than it had for his mother, but finally it sank in.

"We'll have to find her," he said at last.

"How?" Jason asked. He didn't need to ask who.

"I don't know," his father admitted.

The weather that evening was warm and pleasant, so the family ate a picnic dinner in the backyard, Jason's parents seated at one side of the table while Jason stood at the other. Jason had to skip the chicken, but ate heartily of everything else.

In fact, he ate far more than usual, and he'd never been a finicky eater.

"There's a lot more of you to feed," his father pointed out. He added thoughtfully, "This could be expensive."

After dinner, they found they had unexpected company—Gus, who had gone home for his own supper, was back with both his sisters.

"See?" Gus said. "I *told* you!"

The two girls stared, goggle-eyed, and Jason felt himself blushing. He had almost forgotten that he wasn't wearing pants, but now he was more aware of it than ever.

"Wow," said Susannah, Gus's older sister.

"Can I have a ride?" asked Ashley, the younger sister.

"I'm not a horse," Jason protested.

"But you're a centaur," Susannah said.

"Oh, *please?*" Ashley pleaded.

Reluctantly, Jason agreed.

It felt very strange to carry first Ashley and then Susannah around on his back; neither of them seemed to weigh much of anything, as his strange new body was much stronger than his old one. Gus helped the girls on and off, but expressed no interest in taking a turn himself.

The evening passed in a blur of walking and trotting about the yard, with one girl or the other on his back, clinging to his waist or shoulders—he had no saddle or stirrups, nor any mane to hold on to.

At last Gus and his sisters departed, and Jason's family went inside, leaving Jason to settle down in his shed. He took a final look around the yard, then closed the door and went to sleep—standing up, because that was the only position he could get comfortable in. He hoped he would wake in the morning entirely himself again, whether standing up or lying down.

Alas, the next morning he was still half equine.

After breakfast his father reported no listings in the *Yellow Pages* under "witches," "enchanters," "sorcerers," "wizards," or "centaurs." The half-dozen entries under "magicians" all sounded like sleight-of-hand stage acts or party performers, but Jason's dad began calling them all in hopes of finding one who was more than that.

Gus's sisters returned that afternoon with some friends. By the end of the day word of

Jason's condition had spread throughout the neighborhood and several surrounding streets, and a photographer from the town newspaper had turned up to take pictures.

By then Jason was confused and tired, and his feet hurt, but he was beginning to enjoy his sudden celebrity.

The next day his parents questioned everyone at the 7-Eleven, but found no one who could lead them to the witch. Back home, Jason had begun charging a dollar apiece for a trot around the block and was tucking a good bit of money away in his shirt pocket.

He let Susannah and Ashley ride for free, though. And sometimes at night he would go out and gallop full speed, just for the joy of running on his new legs.

By the end of the week Jason and his parents had run out of ideas for locating the witch—or, for that matter, *any* witch or miracle worker. An attempted exorcism by a cooperative priest (most had refused to consider the idea) had done nothing at all, nor had the few strange rituals performed by various self-proclaimed magicians helped.

"I'm sure she'll turn up eventually," Jason's father said.

Jason wasn't so sure.

On the other hand, he was now a genuine celebrity, charging a dollar just to get into the backyard for a close look at him and five dollars for a ride.

The crowds were not really much fun, and most of his friends stayed away rather than be jostled.

"What's it *like?*" people would ask, and Jason could only shrug and say, "I don't know."

It was all very strange and confusing.

And Monday, Jason remembered as he settled to sleep on Saturday night, was the first day of the new school year.

"I'll have to wear shoes," he reminded his mother the next day.

"Well, we could call a farrier. . . ." she said hesitantly.

"I am *not* going to have anything nailed to my toes!" Jason answered.

"Horses don't seem to mind."

"I'm not a horse! And what if I change back?"

"I suppose you're right," she agreed. "Maybe I can make something."

"What about pants?" Jason asked.

"I don't see how," she said. "I mean, if they insist, I'll try, but let's try it without first, all right, Jason?" She glanced involuntarily at his chestnut flank.

Jason sighed. "All right." Getting used to walking around in public without pants had been the hardest part of this whole experience, but he had to admit, when he thought about it, that he would look really stupid wearing anything below the waist—except maybe a blanket. He refused even to consider a saddle.

The shoes his mother came up with were more like bags with drawstrings than like ordinary shoes, but they worked reasonably well.

Jason was incredibly nervous as he walked to school—obviously, he couldn't ride the bus. The first day of junior high, and here he was, half human, half horse—as if starting at a new school wasn't bad enough!

He collected a crowd as he walked, and by the time he reached the school fifty or sixty people were following him, chattering in amazement.

The principal was standing by the front door, greeting the students as they arrived. When Jason trotted up he stared, then shouted, "Hey! You can't come in here!"

"But I'm a student," Jason protested. "I'm registered! Look, I'm in Ms. Hecate's homeroom!" He pointed to the class list posted by the door. "And I'm wearing a shirt and shoes."

The principal hesitated, glanced at the class list, looked back at Jason, then smiled.

"Ms. Hecate?" he said.

Jason nodded.

"All right, then," the principal said. "But try not to cause any trouble."

"Yes, sir." Jason clopped past. The bottoms

were already wearing out of his homemade shoes, and his hooves were loud on the tile floor.

He wondered whether Susannah was right and the teachers were geeks. He wondered how this Ms. Hecate would react to having a centaur in her class.

He was *tired* of being a centaur; he really wished he hadn't mouthed off to that witch. If he ever found her and got turned back, he promised himself, he wouldn't horse around like that again.

He made his way down the school corridor, jostling through the crowd of students, until he reached Room 8. He ducked his head, stepped inside—and froze.

At the teacher's desk stood a woman: Ms. Hecate, presumably. She was dressed in a ratty floor-length black gown that would need cleaning to qualify as filthy. Her greasy, waist-length black hair was unbelievably tangled, and her pointed black hat was absurdly tall. Her nose was spectacularly long and crooked.

She smiled at him. "You must be Jason. I believe we've met before."

Jason swallowed. "Yes, ma'am," he squeaked. He wondered what she was going to do. Was she still mad at him about the insults? Was she going to finish the job of turning him into a horse?

She considered him thoughtfully for a moment, then said, "For today, I'd like you just to stand at the back, if you don't mind."

Jason nodded.

Then Ms. Hecate added, "But tomorrow, bring a pair of pants, and your shoes, and we'll get you into a regular seat."

Jason smiled with relief. "Yes, ma'am!"

Well, he thought, at least *one* teacher wasn't a geek. It was going to be an interesting year.

A gift can be a very heavy burden.

WINDWOOD ROSE

Janni Lee Simner

Draw near, and I'll tell you a story. It's not a story your parents have told you, sitting on the edge of your bed some winter past. If they knew it once, they've probably forgotten. And who could blame them, busy with children of their own, if they quickly lost the magic of the still, soft snow on a long winter night? Not I, and not the girl of the story.

Her name was Miranda Windwood Rose—a fine name on paper, but another thing entirely when said out loud. When all three of her names were spoken at once, they turned hollow and strange, echoing through the air around them like wind through thick leaves. Sometimes the air tried to answer, whispering back in a language Miranda didn't understand.

For her first few years only Miranda's parents spoke her full name, and not knowing anything else, Miranda accepted it easily enough. But on the first day of school, when her teacher read slowly, "Miranda? Miranda Windwood Rose?" things were different. The teacher hesitated at the sudden rustling whisper that filled the classroom; the other children looked around nervously. Miranda knew then that her name wasn't the sort she could carry to school with her year after year. She looked down at her desk and muttered, "Just Randy, please." Her teacher wrote something in her book, the whispering stopped, and that was the end of it.

Miranda feared her parents would be angry and maybe a little hurt at her decision. But Miranda's parents knew that names have magic in them, and that hidden names have more magic than most. They smiled when Miranda said she'd asked to be called Randy; they even followed the teacher's lead and called her the same. They knew that her real name would still be there, waiting for her, whenever she was ready to claim it.

So the whispering went away, at home and at school. The music, however, was harder to leave behind.

Miranda's father played guitar with wild, fierce fingers; her mother sang with a low, steady voice. Miranda fell asleep each night with their music in her ears, and more often than not it shaped her dreams. Some nights she dreamed she danced to her father's guitar in a bright yellow field, and as she danced the tall grass made way beneath her feet. Other nights she dreamed she listened to her mother's singing beside a swift stream, and when Miranda stared at the water it swirled beneath her gaze, as if a large stone lay just beneath the surface. Still other nights she didn't remember her dreams at all, only that as long as music ran behind them, their landscapes changed for her.

When Miranda was very young, the music comforted her. Many nights she stayed up listening and fell asleep in her mother's lap or at the foot of her father's chair. She looked forward to seeing where each night's dreaming would take her.

But at school the rhythm of the music jarred against the rhythms of the schoolyard, with its creaking swing sets and jump rope rhymes. Sometimes, out on the black asphalt, a snatch of music pulled her away, to some strange hillside in some far-off land. When she returned, the other children would be looking at her and laughing.

"What's wrong with you?" a boy asked once, the year that Miranda turned eight. He was an ordinary child, with pale blue eyes and the not-at-all unusual name of Robert.

"Nothing's wrong," Miranda said.

"You don't answer when people talk to you,"

Robert insisted. "Or when you do answer, you stare at them funny. You have really creepy eyes, you know?"

When Miranda went home that night, she stood by the mirror for a long time, staring at her own eyes. They were black and very deep, and when she looked at them too long she got dizzy. When she looked even longer, she saw the fragments of her dreams swirling around in their depths. She heard music, too: not her mother's singing or her father's guitar, but a new tune—like a wooden flute or a deep-running stream—that somehow belonged to her alone.

She blinked once and the dreams faded; she blinked twice and they were gone. She was glad of it. She suddenly wasn't so sure she wanted to have strange dreams or hear strange music. Somehow she knew that no odd dreams lay behind the other children's eyes. She didn't know whether that meant something was wrong with her or something was wrong with them, but all at once the music scared her.

She tried to ask her parents about it. But her parents weren't like other parents, any more than Miranda was like other children. They didn't give the answers other parents would give.

"What am I seeing?" she asked her father one night, as he sat by the fire and carved a small wooden box with patterns of flowers, some flowers Miranda knew, others that she'd never seen. He sold his carvings sometimes, though just as often he decided to keep them once he was through.

Her father didn't answer with words. Instead he set the box aside and stared at her through eyes that were sharp and flickering blue. Then he lifted his guitar from near the hearth and played. Miranda saw fields of wildflowers, swaying even though the air around them was still; she saw distant white clouds racing across a wide sky. She forced herself back to the room, focusing on the fire and the flickering flames. Her father set down the guitar, returned to his carving, and didn't say anything more.

"What am I hearing?" she asked her mother one bright morning, while her mother knelt in the garden and planted spring vegetables. Her mother didn't look at her, but as she continued planting she sang. Miranda saw the sun setting over lush, tree-filled mountains, trailing streamers of light in every color imaginable and a few others besides. She heard music somewhere inside her—the same hollow, wooden music she'd heard at the mirror.

She turned and fled, covering her ears as she ran to her room. The music only grew louder. Her mother didn't follow to see what was wrong; she just quietly turned back to her planting.

Miranda lay awake most of the night, and many nights after, but though she didn't dream, the music wouldn't go away. It couldn't go away, for it wasn't really music at all; it was magic. Her parents knew this, but they never sat down on the edge of Miranda's bed and explained it to her. They knew that magic doesn't make more sense when you try to explain it. Magic needs to take root on its own, to grow slowly and steadily until one day the young mage suddenly says, "Oh, of course," and wonders why she didn't realize all along.

At least, that's how it worked when Miranda's parents were children. But they had lived in a different land then, one where mages were as common as oak trees. No one needed to talk about magic, and it wasn't very frightening at all.

Miranda was as scared of being strange and different as of the music in her head. She did her best to fit in; she watched the other children closely and imitated them. But someone who's so afraid of missing a step that her eyes are always on the person in front of her is never truly graceful. Miranda grew into a quiet, tentative girl. The other children laughed less as she got older, but they never felt very comfortable around her. None of them counted her among their close friends, to write notes to in class, or talk with on the way home from school, or whisper secrets with late into the night.

At fourteen Miranda was tall and thin, with dark hair and darker eyes, which were quite beautiful if you could bear to look at them. That year her birthday fell on the last day before Christmas vacation. As she sat in one class after another, struggling to focus on her teachers and not on the music, snow started falling outside. By noon the world was blanketed in white. By two o'clock the snow was so deep that the school sent everyone home.

Now, I never said there was no magic in our world, only that there weren't any mages. Magic here isn't woven into people. It's woven into the stars, strung across the sky; it's woven into the waterfalls that flow year after steady year, wearing jagged rocks smooth. It's woven into the snow—especially the first snow, falling on the shortest day of the year. So what happened to Miranda next didn't happen only because of her magic. It happened because of the earth's magic, though she never knew that.

As she walked across the schoolyard, coat drawn tight against the wind, the swaying gray branch of a bare tree caught her eye. There was music in that branch, and Miranda stopped, startled. She'd never heard the music anywhere but in her mother's voice and her father's playing and her own head. Then she got angry. It was the beginning of vacation, and she wanted to go home like everyone else, to fall backward onto her bed and count the days until Christmas. She forgot, for the moment, that on short winter nights her parents played their music more loudly than usual.

Miranda looked fiercely away, but the schoolyard was gone, the world a white field bordered only by trees. No breeze stirred the winter afternoon.

You or I would have turned and run then, searching desperately for home, for someone to set the world back in its proper place. But Miranda was sick of being haunted by strange dreams. She stood as tall as she could, threw her head back, and opened her mouth. She meant to demand that whatever had snatched her away send her back at once and keep the music for itself. What came out, though, was that very music . . . a deep hollow tune that echoed across the field. Miranda pressed her lips back together and looked wildly around.

Standing in front of her—so close she didn't know how she'd missed it, so still she didn't know how she saw it, even then—was a silver-white creature, glistening like the dew that catches the first rays of morning sun before it dissolves into day. But the sun was setting, and instead of dissolving the creature solidified,

until its large silver eyes met Miranda's dark ones.

No horn sprang from the animal's forehead, but you'll have to believe me when I say it was a unicorn. I know no other word for a creature that steps so lightly on the crystal snow, not for lack of weight, but because somehow both creature and snow are bound by the same magic.

Miranda had never seen anything so beautiful, in her dreams or out of them. She stared at the creature, not daring to breathe, afraid she'd scare it away. Then she shivered and all her breath rushed from her at once. Instead of running, the unicorn let out a high, silver laugh, a laugh that held the same music as the gray branch, as her mother's singing, as her father's guitar. At the sound of the music Miranda forgot the creature's beauty and grew angry all over again.

The unicorn dropped its gaze, then raised it again, looking Miranda over from her gray boots to her dark hair. "Miranda Windwood Rose," it said, in a serious voice that didn't match its laugh at all.

The air grew even stiller, as if holding its breath and waiting for the answer to some question. Very far away, Miranda heard a sound like whispering leaves.

She pushed her hands deep into her pockets. "No," she said. "Just Randy."

The unicorn stared at Miranda for a while, and Miranda dared not fidget before it. Somehow she knew the slightest movement would upset some balance that could never be set right again. The unicorn lifted one hoof and set it down; the balance was upset after all. Miranda looked to the sparkling snow.

"Miranda Windwood Rose is a good name," the creature said, its words brittle in the chill air. "It is a magic name."

"I don't want a music name," Miranda said, for she hadn't heard quite right.

The unicorn tilted its head. "You can't use magic without a proper name."

"I don't want any magic," Miranda said, for this time she'd heard right. And though she still knew nothing about magic, she understood from the unicorn's words that magic was somehow linked to music, and she knew that she didn't want music.

The unicorn snorted, blowing out frosty air. "The magic is already yours. I can't do anything about that."

"Can't you?" As Miranda spoke, she feared it was a silly thing to say. Then she met the unicorn's serious eyes, and she knew it wasn't silly after all.

"You don't know what you ask," the unicorn said.

But Miranda knew exactly what she asked. She asked for friends—real friends, the kind who could understand her and whom she could understand. She asked for a chance to walk easily and comfortably through the world, without fear of being snatched away by music or magic. She asked for silent dreams.

The unicorn stared at her for a while, and she felt embarrassed, alone beneath its silent gaze.

"I'll hold it for you," the unicorn said at last. "In case you ever want it back."

"I won't want it back," Miranda whispered.

The unicorn looked down its long nose at her. "I'll hold it just the same." It met her eyes with its large silver eyes one last time. Miranda had the uncomfortable feeling that it was pulling something from her, through her eyes, pulling something out of her and making that something its own. She was about to flinch away when the unicorn lifted its head and looked to the darkening sky.

She followed that gaze, and as she stared at the faint stars the world was suddenly, wonderfully silent. She knew then that whatever the unicorn did had worked. The music was gone.

The unicorn turned without speaking and walked toward the edge of the white field. She stared after it. It was still pretty, but not nearly as beautiful as before. She wondered what had changed.

"Wait," she called, and the creature looked hopefully back, ready to return what it had just taken.

"What kind of a name is Randy?" she asked.

"It is an earth name," the unicorn said, but before she could ask whether an earth name was a good name or not, it turned again and jumped, and as it lifted into the air it became the gray branch of a tree, blowing in the evening sky.

And Randy, kicking a drifting whorl of snow out of her path, walked across the schoolyard, a girl like any other girl, on the first day of Christmas vacation.

As soon as she walked in the door, her parents knew. Her father reached out to hug her, then pulled away, seeing nothing but his own reflection in his daughter's eyes. Her mother just stared at her out of deep, dark eyes suddenly so unlike Randy's shallow brown ones. Randy looked at them both, and she smiled; for the first time in a long time, their gazes didn't frighten her.

She started toward her room, her steps quick and light. Behind her, she heard her mother crying. Randy stopped halfway up the stairs. She'd only given up what was hers to begin with, but she suddenly felt like she'd taken something from her parents, too.

She almost ran back out into the snow then, to find the unicorn and say that she wanted the music back, that she would be Miranda Windwood Rose. But instead she kept climbing the stairs. She lay down on her bed, looked up at the ceiling, and heard only her own silent thoughts. And she knew she didn't really regret her decision after all.

The unicorn did as it had promised: it held Randy's magic for her. She never claimed it, though she thought about it sometimes, flinching at her mother's tears or her father's sad eyes. Their music was dull to her now, just one empty note following another, nothing more.

But then, slowly at first, she began talking with the other children at lunch, walking with them on the way home from school. Her quiet, tentative step gave way to an easy laugh, and she decided she didn't have time to waste searching for unicorns.

All of this happened a long time ago. But somewhere, a unicorn still canters through the snow, waiting for Randy to take her magic back.

Maybe now you're thinking that you'd like to walk in the snow, in hopes that some wild gray branch will catch your eye and a unicorn will appear beneath the silver moon. Indeed, if you went out on a night like tonight, a night that follows both the first snow and the shortest day of the year, you might find a unicorn. And if it were the right unicorn, it might offer you the magic Randy never claimed.

Your eyes light up at this. But I hope you'd think well before you accept. For though some magic would be a nice thing to have, silent dreams are nice, too. I don't know which is better. I do know that neither should be cast lightly aside.

For this time, I think, the unicorn would not take the magic back again.

There are many paths to heaven.

BEAR AT THE GATE

Jessica Amanda Salmonson

The little teddy bear was surprised to find himself whole. He had both his button eyes, all his limbs, and felt well stuffed with sawdust. He stood before an enormous gate, gazing up. Around him drifted clouds. The staircase shined of pearl.

The gate opened and a winged man looked out. "Who is this little fellow?" asked St. Peter.

"I'm Henry," said the bear.

St. Peter went away for a moment, then returned with a book, running a delicate finger down the list.

"Just Henry?" he asked.

"Yes."

"Well, there's no Henry listed here. I'm not certain you can enter."

"Enter where?" asked Henry. "I'm not sure I'd want to, really. What's it like?"

"It's not perfect," said St. Peter. "But it's paradise."

"Oh, I think I understand," said Henry, suddenly aware. "I must be dead and this is Heaven. I thought it was odd that I had all my limbs back."

"Hmmm." Peter was thinking. "It's highly irregular to get a stuffed toy at the gate; but clearly yours is an authentic soul. Not all toys have souls, you understand. How did you come to die?"

"Torn limb from limb by an impish boy," said Henry. "Alas! I was an antique bear and had been well cared for, although I lost my eye early on. . . ." (Here he felt upward with his paw, still surprised to have both eyes.) "I hadn't been played with for a long time but had remained stored away in a secret place so that the Old Man could take me out from time to time and look at me. When the Old Man died, most of his stuff was thrown away; it wasn't worth much. As for me, the Old Man's daughter and son-in-law tossed me to the Old Man's grandson, like an old rag tossed to a dog. I think he rather liked me a bit; but he had a funny way of showing it. He tore my arms off and stabbed me with a jackknife, and my sawdust spilled out on the floor."

"Hmmm," said St. Peter once again. "That

was an unfortunate end. Yet nothing in your story explains how you came to sprout a soul."

"I'm sure I never knew I had one," said Henry.

"Well, tell me how you lived—before you were stored away, that is."

"Oh, I had a grand time. When the Old Man was a toddler, he got me for Christmas. He wasn't much bigger than me and crawled more than he walked. He dragged me around with him. I lost my eye before New Year's, but the sensitive child was so alarmed that he was awfully careful after that and treated me terribly well. When he was about sixteen he decided he was a bit old for a teddy bear and put me on a high shelf. When he got married he put me in a box. When he became a widower, he put the box in the attic. I'd gotten tattered over the years and had a few patches, but I was still a stout little fellow." He looked himself up and down, finding no evidence of the wear and tear or the scars of repair.

Still, Peter saw no excuse for a soul, and asked, "Tell me your three strongest memories," for this was a sure test.

Henry wrinkled up his brow and said: "My earliest memory is of that Christmas when I first got hugged. That was awfully nice."

"And your second strongest memory?"

"When I first got put away. That was awfully sad."

"And in between?"

Henry acted as though he didn't want to say.

"What is it?" Peter urged, still standing in the gate, his huge wings spreading out behind.

"It was when the Old Man was eight."

"And?"

"He got sick."

Henry was *very* reluctant to say more.

"You felt bad about that?" said Peter.

"Very bad. He had a terrible fever, and he died."

"He died?" Peter raised a brow. "Then how did he come to be the Old Man?"

"Well, you see, his fever was awful, and he started imagining things. He imagined I was alive and walking around. 'Dearest Henry,' he said to me, 'my throat is so dry, and I need a glass of water.' He was very pitiful, and I just had to get him a glass of water, only I couldn't. Later on he said, 'Dearest Henry, I don't feel nice.' And that's when I found the strength to put my paws around his neck and nuzzle his face just so. I could feel the pulse through the vein of his neck. I felt it stop entirely, and I knew he was dead. 'Do come back,' I whispered. 'Do come back.' And as I said it in his ear very softly, his pulse began anew, the fever broke, and he got better."

"My," said St. Peter. "That was wonderful of you to care so much. Obviously that is how you gained your soul, and that is why you're here at this gate. Still, it is *highly* irregular. There aren't many toys walking around in here. . . . Oh, just a minute."

St. Peter went away again, leaving the gate ajar. Henry heard someone talking to St. Peter, and St. Peter whispering back. Then the gate began to open all the way. There stood a little boy with shining, happy eyes. "Old Man!" cried Henry, and ran into the young boy's arms. "Henry!" said the Old Man, and carried the bear into paradise.

St. Peter shrugged his wings and shoulders, then closed the gate.

When you've spent your life granting others' wishes, it can be hard to figure out exactly what you want for yourself.

THE FOURTH WISH

Nina Kiriki Hoffman

I stood on the corner and waited for Annie to come out of the school. I had known her two weeks, and I would have to leave her soon, because I could feel myself becoming what she wished.

A thousand years I had been trapped in a clay jar, in a sleep troubled by dreams of sand, broken only by a few brief bright moments when someone opened the jar and brought me out into another new era, and then only long enough for them to decide on their wishes.

My final mistress had been a museum curator whose first wish was financial security for the rest of her days, and whose second wish was to own a perfect piece of pottery from ancient Cathay. Those two simple things had satisfied her. Her third wish granted me freedom, since she could think of nothing else she wanted. In the three years since she had made her third wish, I had wandered the world, seeing how it had changed, studying what people had made of it, wondering where I wanted to be in it.

A flood of children burst from the school. Black-eyed Annie came last, staring at the ground and scuffing her shoes. Her stockings were droopy and her shoelaces untied. Dirt smudged her face. Her need was the brightest thing about her. Her need had drawn me to her two weeks earlier as I walked these streets, watching people and tasting the colors of their wishes, telling myself that I was free of all that, though I no longer knew what to do with freedom. I had let Annie's need shape me into a girl a little older than herself, someone she would not fear, someone she could talk with.

She walked past me without looking up. I touched her shoulder. "Annie?"

"Zara! You came!" Her smile lighted her face.

"I said I would."

She bit her lip, nodded, and slid her small hand into mine. We walked together.

The air was cool and damp this day, the sky host to clouds. "Look, Annie. Flowers." I pointed to purple and yellow flowers growing low to the ground in a square of soil that had a tree in its center. "Leaves." I pointed to the dead-looking branches of a tree with baby leaves just emerging from their buds. Where I grew up, long ago and far away, I had not known plants like these that died and resurrected themselves.

She pointed to the flowers. "Crocuses," she said. She had been teaching me the names of things in her language ever since I had met her down by the train tracks.

After two blocks we came to her building. She unlocked the front door and pulled me in. We climbed three flights of stairs to her apartment, where she listened at the door. Only once had she heard something, and then she had sent me away. "Papa doesn't like for me to have friends over," she had whispered.

She straightened today and gave me her best smile, then unlocked the door. "Are you hungry?" she asked.

"Yes," I decided.

"Want crackers?"

"What are crackers?"

"You're so funny!" she said. Her laugh was like a bird's trill. She led me past the sagging couch and the table covered with full ashtrays and dirty dishes. We went into the kitchen. More dishes with food still on them filled the sink and covered the counters. A faint flicker of my lost humanity shuddered through me. Where I grew up we learned about all the things that polluted the body and the household, and our task was to make clean and holy again everything we could, smoking our clothes and our hair with incense, rubbing aromatic oils into our bodies.

But that was a long time ago, and I had seen many ways of living since. People had many different ways of cleansing, or of living with their dirt. I wouldn't want to live with dirt like this.

Annie stood on a chair and got an orange box from a cupboard. "Cheesies," she said, opening the box and offering me the opportunity to reach first into the waxed bag inside. I pulled a cracker out. It was a small, hard, flat orange thing. I smelled it, and it smelled like nothing I had ever tasted. I bit it. It was strange.

Annie grabbed a handful of crackers and stuffed them all into her mouth at once. She chewed and swallowed. Carrying the box, she led me back to the other room, where we sat on the couch. Her hunger had been part of her need landscape; I was glad to see it fading.

"You want to study with me today?" she said. "Today I'll teach you spelling!"

"All right," I said. I could have wished knowledge of written and spoken English into myself, but I liked having Annie teach me.

English shapes of letters were different from Persian. And she loved the letters, loved them with all the passion in her that found nothing else to embrace.

As the light filtering in through the curtains grew yellower and then turned to dark, she showed me things in books, taught me spelling, glowed when I thanked her. She looked often at the clock on top of the television, though, and when it was nearly eight she stood up. "Time for you to leave," she said. Her need said, *stay, stay, stay.*

Her wish whispered: *I wish you were my sister.*

Before, I had only an idea of the shape of the wish, but today I could feel every word of it. If I stayed near it any longer, it would print itself into me in the language of the heart.

"Thank you for the crackers," I said, and left.

I went to the park by the river and watched the green-gray water for a long time, watched the way the ripples set themselves in braided patterns. I could be formed and set like that, locked in a pattern, and it would be hard for me to break free. Annie didn't even need to voice her wish; my whole being had been tuned to listen for wishes.

If I became her sister, it would be as if I had always been her sister, living in that dirty place with her, subject to the same forces that had shaped her.

I loved her in a way I had never loved anything before, but I did not want that.

I left. I flew away from the city to the top of a snow-skinned mountain, where I could not feel anyone's wishes. It was a chill and sicklemooned night.

I took the shape of a fire-bellied sky lizard, like those I had seen in tapestries in Cathay. The cold did not bother me because I held heat inside.

I could stay here in the mountains, far from the colors of need and desire. I could go home to the deserts of my birth and live out my days under the hot, heavy hand of the sun. Live out my days. Who knew how long a span that would be? I could take the form of a creature from the deeps and live far beneath the surface of the ocean. I could go to another city and wander free until someone else's need spoke to me . . . and little Annie would walk home alone and wonder where Zara had gone, or if she had ever been there at all. I could take the memory of me from Annie's mind, but I didn't want to do that; she had so many unpleasant memories, and I knew she liked the ones of me.

My fire belly was melting the snow I lay upon. Tiny rivers ran down the mountain away from me, only to freeze lower down. Beneath my scaled skin I felt stone.

I could explain things to Annie, tell her she could wish for something, anything but that I become her sister. She could wish for me to take her away; she could wish she lived in some other house, with some other family; she could wish she were grown up, or a dragon, or a mountain; I could give her jewels and riches and a palace if she pleased. But what if she made the wrong wish? People often did.

I spent all night curled around the mountain, watching the moon and stars move across the heavens as they had done for centuries, changing course but a little, with no regard to the lives played out below. I could become the moon and not care any longer what happened to anyone. . . .

In the light of early dawn I looked down at my form. I had thought myself beyond the reach of any need, but I realized that I, too, wore a cloak of wishes: peacock green, silver, copper, fire orange, the green of spring leaves, red the color of blood.

I could make a wish.

I had never made a wish.

People often made the wrong wish.

I waited for Annie on the corner. This time she was one of the first out, and she looked up

and saw me right away. Smiling, she came and held out her hand for mine.

"I have to talk to you," I said.

Her smile disappeared, replaced by a troubled frown. I led her over to a bench where people waited for buses, and we sat down. She looked up at me, her black eyes bright and wide.

"Would you like to be my sister?" I asked.

Her face lit up.

To make a good wish, you have to plan very carefully. I had seen many wishes go bad, mostly ones that concerned forcing other people to love you or to become what you loved.

"I would like you to be my sister," I said. "Then you could be like me. I don't want to be your sister because I don't want to be like you."

She blinked. Her smile faded.

"I'm explaining this badly," I said. "If I become your sister, I would live with you and your papa. If you became my sister, you would be different, the way I am. No longer human—free of so many things that rule you now. We could live wherever we wanted. We could live in a different place every day, or we could stay in one place for a hundred years. We could go to the moon."

"You can go to the moon?" she said softly.

"To the moon. To the other side of the world. To the center of the earth, with just a wish." I opened my free hand and showed her a lavender wish, soft and glowing.

Her eyes widened. She glanced from my wish to my face and back. She reached out to touch the wish, but instead closed her hand and held it curled against her chest. "I can't leave Papa," she said. "Who would cook for him? Who would wake him up in time to get to work?"

"We could arrange to have a hot meal appear every day for him, if you like. We could leave him a special talking alarm clock. We could even leave him a doll that looks like you and cooks meals and wakes people up, but is not alive and never feels hungry or alone. We could make him comfortable. We wouldn't have to be there."

"You could make a doll that looks like me? One that he couldn't tell wasn't me?" she asked.

"He could tell if he really, really looked at her," I said.

She licked her lip and stared at a pink blob of gum on the sidewalk. "He'll never notice," she whispered.

I held her hand and waited.

Presently she looked up at me and asked, "Would I go to school?"

"Do you want to?"

She was quiet for a little while, but then she

said, "I love Mrs. Henderson. I want to see her every day."

"You can go to school as long as you like. You could teach me everything you learn, or I could look younger and go to school with you. We can live anywhere we like and have good food every day. On weekends we can go to the ends of the earth."

She looked up at me, and after a moment she smiled. "I want to be your sister."

We live in a place hidden in the Himalayas. We have fresh, ripe fruit all year, and blankets made of spider silk and stuffed with down from clouds. Every morning I take Annie back to her school in the United States, though she has learned how to travel by herself, and every afternoon I wait on the street corner for her to come out. Her cheeks have roses in them now, and she always starts the day with her hair combed and her clothes clean, though she usually doesn't end up that way.

The only thing that worries me is that she has begun to notice the color of other people's wishes. Yesterday she told me about a ragged little boy she sees in kindergarten.

She wants us to walk him home.

One of the basic rules of magic is that names have power and importance.
Which doesn't make a weird name any easier to live with.

BYRD SONG

Nancy Springer

"I could just *die,*" Phoebe wailed at the gloomy hemlock forest. Nobody else was around, or at least she hoped not. She had walked far into the woods to be alone with her unhappiness. "I could just eat worms and die. They couldn't call me anything *normal,* noooo, they had to go and call me Phoebe. *Fee-Beeee.*" She whined the name. She hated it. "Why didn't they call me Chickadee and have it over with?"

What had her parents been thinking? They should have known a kid named Phoebe Byrd would get picked on. Then of course her father had to be an ornithologist, which made things worse, and he had to write his stupid book, *Byrd's Birds.* Now he'd moved the family to northern Pennsylvania for a year so that he could study the hawk migration. And the kids at the new school were having fun, fun, fun with Phoebe.

"Everybody hates me." Phoebe plopped to the ground under the dark, shaggy trees and started to cry.

"Squonk." Muffled sobbing noises sounded through the hemlocks. *"Squonk."*

At first Phoebe thought it was her. Then she stiffened to listen and stopped crying, but the noises went on.

"Squonk. Squ-squ-squoooonk."

"Who's there?" Phoebe whispered.

The sobbing abruptly stopped.

"Who is it?" Phoebe asked. "Somebody was crying and it wasn't me."

"Squonk," said the weeper, rustling the bed of fallen needles under the next hemlock tree.

Through the branches Phoebe could see enough empty space to show her that what she was hearing could not possibly be a person. The squonker couldn't be any bigger than a chicken. "Oh, for—you're some sort of weird bird, aren't you?" And she, Phoebe Byrd, who of all people should know a bird when she heard one, was sitting there talking to it. She had to laugh at herself. "Oh, for crying out loud." Then she realized what she had said and laughed again.

"Don't laugh at me." The Squonk sniffled. *"Squonk."*

"Squonk to you, too," Phoebe replied automatically before she sat straight up and gawked. "No, you're not a bird!" Birds didn't talk, except maybe parrots, and even parrots couldn't have a real conversation with a person. "Who are you? Where are you?" Was somebody playing tricks?

"I am too a bird," said the Squonk, hurt feelings moistening every word. "Don't make fun of me. *Squonk.*"

"But . . . you talk?"

"Why not? You were talking to nobody. I am at least talking to you."

Where the hemlock boughs hung thickest Phoebe thought she could see a shadow about the size of a quail. From the same place came the sound of the Squonk sniveling through its beak. Okay, it was a talking bird, which was weird and scary—but it was hard to feel terrified of anything so weepy. Instead, Phoebe felt curious.

"Come out where I can see you," she coaxed.

"*Squooooonk!* No! Absolutely not! *Squ-squ-squ—*"

"Okay, okay!"

"I'm shy," the Squonk apologized, hiccuping. "I embarrass easily."

"Talk about embarrassed." Phoebe leaned

toward the shadowy Squonk. "Today was the worst day of my life."

"The only reason I am talking with you at all," the Squonk stated plaintively, "is that you were squonking and I thought you might be another one of me."

But Phoebe was intent on the story of her bad day. "They invited my father to do an assembly at school today," she told the Squonk, "and there in front of the whole school he has to go and say he named me after his favorite bird. Why does he have to say stuff like that? Everybody laughed. Everybody looked at me. Now kids I don't even know are picking on me. All day it's been nothing but 'Fee-Bee's a birdbrain' and 'Feeb, do you lay blue eggs?' and all sorts of gross, stupid jokes and they won't stop. I just want to crawl into a hole and never come out."

"Squonk," the bird wept. Phoebe could not tell whether it had been listening to her or not, but its sobbing made her feel better, as if it were doing the crying for her. *"Squ-squ-squooonk."*

"What are you crying about?" Phoebe asked gently. Just talking with the Squonk was making her forget her own troubles and feel sorry for it instead.

"Because I am going to *die. Squoooooonk!"*

Phoebe sat up straight. This was a problem

slightly bigger than hers. "You mean, as in become dead?" she whispered. "Like, soon?"

"C-c-could be." The Squonk's voice struggled through its weeping.

"But . . . why?" Phoebe wondered if it had some sort of awful disease.

"Just . . . because . . . I am a . . . *Squooooooooooooooooooonk!*"

The Squonk was bawling too hard to talk now. "Oh, poor Squonk," Phoebe murmured. She got on her hands and knees and started crawling toward it under the hemlock boughs to try to comfort it.

"No!" the Squonk shrieked. "No! *Squonk!* No! *Squonk!* No! *Squonk!*" Phoebe heard it scuttle away under the hemlocks. It must have been a flightless bird. She peered through the trees, but saw not a feather of it as its squonking faded into the distance.

"Poor Squonk," she whispered to herself, sorry that she had frightened it. She got up to go home, and then she saw the place where the Squonk had been hiding. Under the lowest hemlock bough shone a puddle of tears.

"Dad," Phoebe asked her father at the dinner table, "have you ever heard of a Squonk bird?" He had brought home pizza for supper since Phoebe's mother was working, and he had apologized to Phoebe several times for what had happened at assembly. Phoebe felt like she ought to forgive him.

"A Squonk!" He smiled all over his round face. "The weeping widgeon. Yes, I've heard of it. It's legendary in this area. The poor thing is supposed to be so ugly it won't show itself, which is a handy quality in a mythical bird."

"Mythical bird?"

"Imaginary. You know, like the Gillygaloo. That's the one that nests on hilltops and lays square eggs. Or, strictly speaking, cubical eggs. If hard-boiled and properly marked, supposedly they can be used for dice."

Phoebe wanted to get the conversation back to the Squonk. "Why does it cry?"

"The Gillygaloo? Wouldn't you? Imagine laying those eggs."

"The Squonk."

"Oh. Self-pity, I suppose. The story goes that it weeps such a spate all the time that it can be tracked by its trail of tears. But if you catch up to it, it dissolves entirely into waterworks. It is the only creature I have ever heard of that can quite literally die of embarrassment."

"Poor Squonk," Phoebe murmured. She knew about embarrassment.

"Now, if it were like the Phoenix it could rise from its ashes. Or rather, from its bubbles." Phoebe's father chuckled.

Phoebe sat silently. She didn't think it was

funny. But she felt a tug at the very back of her brain, as if something were calling her. She thought about the Phoenix. She thought about the Squonk. And she knew what she would do.

The next day when she was supposed to walk to the school bus stop, Phoebe walked instead into the hemlock forest. She had made herself an extra big lunch—three peanut-butter-Swiss-cheese-pickle-and-potato-chip sandwiches, her favorite—and stowed it in her jacket pockets. She left her bookbag under a tree.

She hiked quickly to the place where she had encountered the Squonk the afternoon before and started searching.

"Hey, Squonk!"

No answer.

The trail of tears it had left under the hemlocks had dried and disappeared. Phoebe went off in the general direction in which the Squonk had run away from her.

"Squonkie!"

No answer.

"This isn't going to work," Phoebe muttered to herself. No way would the Squonk answer. She was being too cheerful.

"Squooonkkk," she began to wail. *"Squosquonk!"*

She forced herself to remember how the kids had picked on her the day before, which made her feel so bad that managing a few squonking sobs was not hard.

"Wonk," she bawled, pinching her nose to make herself sound even more pitiful. *"Squ-squ-squ—"*

"Stop it!" somebody equally pitiful bawled back. "Stop mocking me! *Squonk!*"

The voice came wetly from a thicket of laurel not far away. Phoebe stood still at once and did not go any nearer. "I'm not mocking," she said. "I was just trying to find you."

"Why? What do you wa-wa-want? *Squooonk!*"

"I just want to talk with you some more."

For a moment the Squonk was silent except for some sniffling and a few hiccups. Phoebe waited.

Sullenly the Squonk asked, "Talk about what?"

"You." Despite her urge to pull aside the leaves and see the bird, Phoebe sat down on the ground right where she was. "Why do you think you are going to die?"

"Because, I . . . *squonk* . . . am so re-duck-ulous, so ugglesome . . ." The realization started the squonk squonking again. *"Wonk! Gwonk! Squooonk!"*

"There are lots of ridiculous birds," Phoebe pointed out. "There are loons and coots and boobies and snipe and limpkins and cuckoos and smews. And there are people with ridiculous bird names, like me. We don't just up and die."

"Birds, people, you all look good compared to—*squonk!*—me," grieved the Squonk. "The moment anybody sees me—*squonk!*—that is the moment I die."

"Anybody? Anything? What if a chipmunk sees you?"

"Squ-squ-squonk! Don't talk about it."

The Squonk was getting very upset, but Phoebe felt she had to press on. "What if another Squonk sees you?"

"There are no other Squonks," this one snuffled. "I'm the only one left."

"But—yesterday you said—"

"I *know,* I thought you *might* be one, but you're *not,* because there *aren't* any."

"Poor Squonk." Phoebe wished she could comfort the lonely bird somehow, but she knew better than to move. "Would you like a sandwich?"

"No, thank you," said the Squonk with deepest soggy rue.

All this misery was making Phoebe hungry. She pulled a sandwich from her lunch bag and took several large bites. That made her feel better. "What do Squonks eat? I mean, what do you eat?"

"Spring water, mostly."

Made sense. With all the eyewash it put

out, the Squonk practically had to live on water. Phoebe nodded and finished her sandwich slowly, thinking.

She asked, "Do you happen to know if there's a Phoenix around here anywhere?"

"Why would there be?" the Squonk asked sulkily.

"I just thought maybe—"

"Don't you know who the Phoenix is?" the Squonk interrupted with great passion, sounding very different than before. "The Phoenix is a daughter of the sun. She lives on the mountaintop of the Uttermost East, *not* on this drab lump of a hill. In a nest of sweetest spices, *not* a shabby forest. Her pinions are jeweled, the feathers of her neck are made of pure gold. What would she be doing here?"

"You're a mythical bird," Phoebe argued. "You're not supposed to exist, but you're right here in little ol' Pennsylvania."

"Squonk," it wept softly. "Yes, I am here, alas and *squonk.*"

Why had it given in so easily? This bird's constant weepiness was starting to annoy Phoebe. "Well, do you want to stay here or not?" she burst out. "I thought maybe the Phoenix could help you. You know, because she lives a long time. I thought if we could find a Phoenix, maybe she could give you some pointers and you wouldn't have to die."

"Why should she?"

"Why not?"

The Squonk was silent. Not even sniffling noises came from the laurel thicket where it hid.

"Squonk?"

"I'm thinking," it muttered.

"Okay." Phoebe pulled out another sandwich and ate it. Occasional soft lamentations from the thicket told her that the Squonk was still there. "What are you thinking?" she ventured after she had finished her sandwich and licked her fingers.

After a long silence, the Squonk said softly, without a single wonk or squonk or hiccup, "I am thinking that I can hear the Phoenix calling. All the birds, all, she is calling to her, because it is her time."

Then Phoebe felt it again: the tug at the back of her mind, the call. Her heart beat faster, like a bird's wings, with excitement.

But—nah. She wasn't a bird.

She said to the Squonk, "Are you going to see her?"

"To reach the Uttermost East, one must fly."

"Oh." Now Phoebe felt dead with disappointment. The Squonk couldn't fly.

"You can take me," the Squonk said.

"I—I can?"

"Yes. S-s-stand up."

Phoebe did it.

"Come dip your fingers in my tears." A shining trickle ran out of the laurel bush. "But don't look at me!" the Squonk added hastily and frantically.

Phoebe went over and wet her fingertips, keeping her gaze on the ground.

"Now, close your eyes, think of the Phoenix, and spread your wings!"

Phoebe didn't do it yet. "What about you, Squonk?"

She heard something patter up behind her. "*Don't* look," the Squonk warned. Then it must have jumped. She felt it land on her shoulder. All she could tell about it was that it was lightweight, bony, and wet. Wet feet gripped her collar, and already tears were trickling down her neck as the Squonk burrowed under her hair. "Now!" it ordered with a sob, right in her ear. "Fly!"

Phoebe closed her eyes, spread her arms, flapped mightily, and knew right away that she wasn't in Pennsylvania anymore.

There were no treetops. There was nothing but pearl-colored cloud. The wind in her face told Phoebe she was flying fast, yet she scarcely seemed to be moving at all. Nothing seemed to be moving, not the clouds, not even time itself.

There was no approach, no landing. Quite suddenly the mountain of the Uttermost East was simply there, with Phoebe standing on its shoulder.

On the mountaintop shone the Phoenix.

In its nest of spices at the end of the earth, the Phoenix sang to the sun her song of completion, and all the birds of water and earth and air had gathered around. Phoebe could tell the mountain peak had to be at the end of the earth because the sun had dipped so near. It hung above the Phoenix's head like a crown of fire, and no one could bear to look at her. Phoebe squinted hard and thought she saw haloed in that glory something like an eagle with a golden breast and wings of shining purple, but then she had to rub her eyes and could not look again.

She felt the Squonk shaking where it huddled at the back of her neck, hidden under her hair. Near her on the mountain's shoulder stood a Gillygaloo, square eggs and all, and a quink goose, and a quetzal. Also there were magpies, dowitchers, cedar waxwings, shoebill storks, godwits, honeycreepers—at least one of every kind of bird there was. They covered the stony mountain like a rainbow cloak. Right next to Phoebe stood a keel-billed toucan and a cassowary. The toucan was staring at her. "You're a strange bird," it remarked.

"Shhh," the cassowary hissed. The toucan shushed. From all the tens of thousands of birds not a chirp rose, not a caw or a hoot, honk or twitter. All stood utterly silent as the Phoenix sang her song, more rare and beautiful than that of any dying swan—for there are many swans, but the Phoenix was the only one of her kind.

Lone, alone, all alone,
Under moon, under sun,
I watch the ocean eat the land,
I watch the rivers run.
I see them slow and fatten,
I see them flow like snakes,
I take them in my talons
And make them straight again.
I watch the mountains feed the sea;
My day of years is done. . . .

Phoebe felt as much as heard sobbing, and it might not even have come from the shy bird nestled under her hair. It might have come from her own throat, the Phoenix was so glorious and fiery and sad.

So again an eon ends,
So I go,
So I come.
Lone, alone, all alone,
Under the moon,
Under the sun.

The sun slipped a little lower. From the Phoenix's nest of spices, smoke began to rise.

"Squonk!" a small voice cried. "No, she is so beautiful, no, she must not die! *Squoooonk!"*

The Phoenix lifted her great wings, and their purple feathers blazed into red flames. Great golden flames surged up from her nest, her funeral pyre, and engulfed her. Spicy smoke filled the air. The Phoenix sang on as she died, but soon no one could hear her, for the Squonk's was not the only voice lifted now. Every bird cried out in sorrow. The mountainside echoed with their cries.

But the Squonk was the only bird that could actually shed tears. And the Squonk was the only bird that moved from its place. Phoebe felt its tiny claws dig into her neck as it sprang away, and then she saw it. There, on the ground, scuttling forward, she saw it for the first time: a small, ducklike creature the icky brown color of a UPS truck and covered with—warts? Some sort of bumps. It was indeed very, very ugly. And it was weeping hard. As it scrabbled across the rocky mountaintop it left a shining trail of tears.

Ten thousand pairs of eyes besides Phoebe's saw it, but it seemed to have forgotten about dissolving into a puddle of self-pity.

"*Squonk,* oh no, oh *squonk,* she was so beautiful," the Squonk grieved. "Oh, she was so beautiful, oh no, oh *squonk.*" Why was it not embarrassed to death? Because it was not thinking about itself at all, Phoebe realized. This might have been the first time ever that it had wept for something other than itself.

"Oh, *squonk, squoooonk,*" it cried as it reached the edge of what had been the Phoenix's nest of spices, where nothing now remained but the hot ashes that had been her.

The sun had shrouded its glory behind the mountain. Muted Phoenix colors, gold and red and purple, clouded the sky.

The Squonk waded into the ashes. Phoebe winced, hoping its ever-wet feet did not feel the heat. Its tears fell on the ashes in big drops—one, two, three, half a dozen. And as each tear fell, with a sound like a sigh a puff of steam rose up.

"Squ-squ-onk," the Squonk mourned. *"Squ—squoooonk?"*

The puffs of steam were condensing into—

"More Squonks!" Phoebe shouted, suddenly happy to her bones. She ran forward. "Little Squonks!" There were brown warty baby Squonks clustering around her Squonk's webbed feet; Squonks springing up from the ashes of the Phoenix and the tears of a Squonk who cared. "Oh, Squonk, how wonderful!"

She picked it up and cuddled it in her arms.

It laid its mud-brown bill against her chest, and no tears rolled from its wide brown eyes at all.

"You are beautiful," she told it, stroking its drab brown feathers and its warts.

"Squaank," the little ones complained at her feet. She looked down, and one of them saw her staring and instantly melted into a tiny pool of tears. But before she could cry out in horror, there it was again, as good as ever, rising from its puddle just the way—

Just the way the Phoenix was rising from its ashes.

The Phoenix.

Rising.

Only a few feet away.

Phoebe started to tremble and sank to her knees. Before her, almost within arm's reach, a new Phoenix was growing. And this time she could see everything. She could see the crown of golden feathers on its head. She could see the purple jeweled sweep of its wings, and its blood-red breast, and its sky-deep eyes, as blue as sapphires, fixed on her.

As hard as sapphires, too.

"Sorry," Phoebe whispered, shaking. One ought to shake when one has ventured far too close to a Phoenix. Hastily Phoebe gathered all the little Squonks into her arms along with the original. "I, uh, I apologize, Your Majesty, we'll all be out of your nest in a minute—"

The Phoenix blinked, and they were out of there even faster than Phoebe expected.

The next instant, Phoebe and her armload of Squonks landed on the soft earth under a familiar grove of hemlock trees. Overhead, the sky glowed sunset colors, Phoenix colors: red, gold, purple. Nearby, a spring seeped out from under a layer of spicy fallen hemlock needles. The Squonklings scrambled out of Phoebe's arms and scuttled there to load up on tear juice, but the Squonk stayed where it was.

"Phoebe!" an anxious voice called not far away.

"Oh, poor Daddy," Phoebe whispered. It was getting late, and he was worried about her.

"Squaaank!" all the little Squonks joined in plaintively. "Fee-Bee! *Squ-squ-squaaank!* Fee-Bee!"

"I've got to go," Phoebe told the Squonk she was still holding in her arms. "You'll be okay. You've got other Squonks to be with now."

"Yes!" She actually heard happiness in its voice. "But come *see* me. Please. Often."

"I will." Phoebe kissed it on its warty head, then put it gently down on the ground.

"Phoebe!" Mr. Byrd sounded about ready to cry.

"I'm right here, Daddy!"

The Squonk stood looking after her as she ran to her father.

* * *

The next day, like a Phoenix rising from the ashes, Phoebe went back to school with her head held high. Phoenix ashes had gotten on her; maybe that was what had made the difference. Or maybe it was the long talk she had had with her father that evening. Or maybe, like the Squonk, she had stopped thinking only of herself.

"Hi, Birdbrain!" somebody greeted her the minute she got on the school bus.

"Hey, Feeb!" yelled somebody else. "Lay any eggs lately? How's life? For the birds?"

Phoebe didn't much care what they said. She wet her lips and puckered them to whistle an I-don't-care tune—but the sounds that came from her mouth were bird calls of such rare beauty that every kid on the bus stopped talking or teasing to listen. The bus driver stopped the bus in the middle of the road to hear. Wild birds—goldfinches and juncos and indigo buntings—flew into the bus through the open windows and perched on the seat backs as Phoebe kept whistling, happy to be alive. From up in the hemlock forest another bird joined in, singing along with her.

"Squonk," it sang. *"Squooooooooonk."*

I always wanted to find a magic shop where you could buy real magic. Finally I invented my own: Elives' Magic Shop, which is the starting point for such books as Jeremy Thatcher, Dragon Hatcher *and* Jennifer Murdley's Toad. *Oddly enough, I started both of those books with the intention that they would be short stories. Then I got carried away.*

Here's a story about someone who visited Mr. Elives' Magic Shop that I did *manage to keep short.*

WATCH OUT!

Bruce Coville

"I'm home!" yelled Kirby Markle, bursting through the front door of his house.

Without waiting for an answer, he pounded up the stairs and dashed into his bedroom. Flopping onto his bed, he tore open the box he had bought at that strange magic shop he found when he took the new shortcut home.

Inside he found a second box. Written across the top in bold black letters were the words

The Cave of the Gnome. Underneath, in smaller green print, it said: Fool Your Family! Amaze Your Friends! A Fascinating Device for Both Amateur and Professional Magicians.

Kirby examined the box with wide eyes. Would this be the trick he finally got to work? Mr. Elives, the weird old man who ran the shop, had said it was especially good for someone like him—someone who was in a real hurry to learn magic.

Fumbling with the tape that held the box shut, he tore open the flaps, then held the box upside down over his bed.

Out tumbled a cave made of papier-mâché.

A look of uncertainty crossed Kirby's face. How was this going to make things disappear?

"Kirby!" called his mother. "Supper!"

Kirby sighed. He didn't want to go to supper now. He wanted to figure out how to make this trick work.

"Just a minute, Mom!"

He began reading the directions.

"Kirby!"

"All right, all right. I'm coming!" Shoving the directions into his pocket, he bolted down the stairs.

As soon as supper was over, Kirby asked his mother and father to come into the living room.

"I have something I want to show you," he said.

He herded them through the door and onto the couch, then raced back upstairs to grab the cave.

"I got a new trick today," he announced as he hurtled back down the steps, two and three at a time.

Kirby's parents exchanged smiles. Kirby wanted so badly to be a magician. But he had never yet gotten a trick to work properly. He was always so eager to show them off that he never took the time to learn how to do them right.

"Did you read the directions yet?" asked his mother gently.

"Sort of," said Kirby. "It's gonna be great. Now, I need something to put in the cave. Can I have your watch, Dad?"

Kirby's father looked properly doubtful. "Will I get it back?" he asked.

"Oh, Dad."

"Well, okay," said his father, smiling. "But be careful with it. It's quite expensive."

He took out his pocket watch and gave it to Kirby.

"Now, watch this," said Kirby. He put the watch in the cave. Then he rolled the little papier-mâché boulder across the front of it. Putting his right hand on the cave, he read the magic words off the instruction sheet, at the same time giving the top a little twist. He smiled to himself. The twist must be what activated the mechanism that would hide the watch.

Boom!

The noise was so loud it actually shook the windows. A puff of smoke rose from the cave, and red flames licked out around the little boulder.

Kirby snatched his hand away. "OW!" he cried.

Mr. and Mrs. Markle looked at each other nervously.

Trying to act casual, Kirby removed the boulder from the front of the cave.

The watch was gone.

"Presto Kazam!" he said with a big smile. "A genuine magical trick!"

Kirby's parents applauded dutifully. But his father had a worried look on his face. "Why don't you bring it back now?" he said gently.

"You bet!" said Kirby. He put the boulder back in front of the cave and twisted the top to the left.

Nothing happened.

He tried it again.

Nothing happened.

He twisted it to the right.

Nothing happened.

Kirby snatched up the directions and began

reading frantically through them. Suddenly he turned very pale.

"What is it, Kirby?" asked his mother.

Without saying a word, Kirby handed her the paper.

Gregory Gnome was puttering about in his cave when he heard the bell ring. A greedy smile crossed his face and he ran to the loading platform.

The smile faded a little. Another gold watch. He'd been hoping for something really valuable. A diamond ring, perhaps.

Well, it's better than a sharp stick in the eye, he thought with a shrug.

He carried the watch, which was nearly as big as he was, to the storage area. Once there, he hoisted it into a box already close to overflowing with watches. He really would have to have a cave sale someday soon to turn some of these watches into usable cash. Trolls liked this kind of thing. Maybe they would buy a few of them.

"Gregory!" snapped a sharp voice behind him. "Aren't you ashamed of yourself, taking advantage of all those children?"

Gregory winced. His face took on an injured expression. As he turned to his wife, he pulled a sheet of paper from his pocket. "Look at

these directions," he said. "Read the last paragraph to me."

It was his wife's turn to sigh. "I don't have to read it. I know it by heart: 'Once an object is placed in the Mystical Cave it can never be returned. Therefore, please be sure to use only objects which have no real value.' "

"Well, there it is," said Gregory, looking soulful. "It could hardly be any plainer, could it? All I wanted to do was give kids a toy they could have some fun with. Can I help it if not one out of twenty of the little weezers is smart enough to read the directions before he tries to use the thing? Can I?"

No matter how hard he tried to look serious, Gregory could not hide the greedy smile that twitched at the corners of his mouth.

The little papier-mâché cave was in tiny pieces all over the Markles' living room floor.

Of papier-mâché there was a lot. Of the gold watch, not a trace.

"Kirby," said Mr. Markle, "come with me. I want to have a little talk with you."

Slowly, very slowly, Kirby followed his father out of the room.

Sometimes magic runs in the family. . . .

THE WONDERWORM

Laura Simms

Jana considered herself "badluck." For instance, in the fifth grade she was daydreaming, staring at something in the distance, not seeing anything, when Mrs. Pearlstein tapped her on the shoulder and accused her of reading Sarah's exam paper. Startled, Jana said, "No. No. I wasn't looking at her paper. I was just staring in that direction." Mrs. Pearlstein didn't believe her. So, Jana grew quiet and said to herself, "Badluck. You are nothing but badluck."

She dreaded school. Sixth grade was the worst, particularly the high socks her mother insisted she wear, which none of the other girls wore; her lisp when she read out loud; and the embarrassment of counting on her fingers in math class. "Badluck," she said to herself.

Jana liked to daydream. It kept her far from the mountain of darkness she felt within herself.

Weekends were better. On the weekends her mother sent her to visit her grandmother in the Bronx. "Spending time with Grandma is very special," her mother explained. Her brother, who was fifteen, took her on the A train, stayed for dinner, and went back to Brooklyn.

Her grandmother, Malka, listened to Jana's imagined stories. And she told her granddaughter her own tales, taught her Hebrew songs and funny riddles, and showed her things. Malka owned a necklace with bear claws; an Egyptian blue bead with a scarab engraved on it; a silver hand with Hebrew letters from Poland where she was born; and a copper gypsy amulet.

"Where did you find the bear claw necklace?" Jana asked.

Her grandmother smiled. "When I was twelve years old, I dreamed that a walrus cut a hole in the ice of the Black Sea and gave it to me. When I awoke, it was beside me."

Whether the tales the old woman told Jana were true or made up was not important. Jana loved to hear them. Listening made her heart beat softly. A cool breeze ruffled the grass on the dark mountain in her soul.

One Sunday as she traveled with her grandma back home to Brooklyn, Jana said, "I dreamed of an antelope running in a field." The old woman assured her, "To dream of an animal is a blessing." That is how they spoke to each other as they rode on the subway.

Malka always carried a small cedar box "for protection." It was the size of her palm. On Friday and Saturday nights, Malka placed it beneath the fold-out cot where Jana slept in the living room. "It keeps away the evil eye, my granddaughter."

For Jana's eleventh birthday, when she became "a young woman," her grandmother told her the most extraordinary story while they were on the A train. So it was that halfway between the Bronx and Brooklyn, she heard the story of what was in the box.

This tale Jana was certain was not factual. However, she had come to understand that "everything that is true is not necessarily fact."

"When I was a little girl in Poland, my mother, may she rest in peace, took me to see a Rebbe in Warsaw because I was always daydreaming. She was afraid a demon would steal my soul when I wasn't paying attention. He was a famous Rebbe, so I wore my best Sabbath dress. He gave me the box. He told me never to open it. I have never opened it. He said, 'It will keep away the evil eye and bring you good luck.' I believed him. It was a very special gift."

Jana spoke loudly over the sound of the train. "Do you know what is in the box?"

Shaking the box lightly, Malka said, "Of

course I know what is inside. I have known for a long time. I saw a picture of it in a Holy Book."

"What was the name of the Book?"

"That I don't remember," said the old woman. "But I know that inside is a copper egg. Inside the copper egg is a silver egg. And inside that little egg is a blue stone, as blue as lapis lazuli. And in that stone is a tiny worm."

"A worm. That's horrible!" shrieked Jana.

Laughing, Malka added, "Not an ordinary worm. A Wonderworm, like the worm that helped King Solomon build the Temple of Jerusalem. And where did he get the worm? He tricked Asmodeus, the King of Demons, who kept it at the bottom of the dark mountain where he lived."

Malka didn't say another word to Jana on the subway. Jana knew she would hear the rest of the story later. They rode silently until they reached her station. Side by side they walked to Jana's house, but didn't enter. Instead, they sat together on the stone steps in front of the porch and talked.

Malka's eyes were half closed as she continued the tale.

"Beautiful child of my daughter, the Wonderworm was made of gold and the flesh of six demons. It was covered with jewels from the flask that held the waters of life. It had two ruby eyes. It had wings, but couldn't fly. It had tiny diamond legs, and it left a path of invisible tears of gold."

Before going into the house, Malka tucked the cedar box into Jana's red plaid overnight bag.

"Now it is yours."

At the dinner table that night, while the family was eating Malka's delicious rose red borscht and platters of cheese blintzes and cucumbers, Malka told a story. She did not mention the box.

"This is just a story for children," she said, including Jana's mother and father in the category of children.

"When King Solomon commanded his builders to make a new Temple in Jerusalem, the stones were too hard to be cut by ordinary men. The Queen of Sheba, the wisest of Solomon's wives, told him the secret. He had to find the Shomir, the Wonderworm. Only the Shomir with its diamond legs could carve the great stones. However, the Wonderworm was owned by Asmodeus, the King of Demons. King Solomon was acquainted with Asmodeus. A wise King, my children, always knows both worlds: the spirit and the human worlds, both evil and good. But a human being, King or no King, could not ask for this worm in an ordinary way. Only the greatest love could retrieve it."

Jana looked around the table and noticed that Malka's storytelling was so good no one was eating.

"Solomon made a plan. He ordered his servants to capture the newly hatched baby of the Rukh."

"What is a Rukh?" asked Jana's brother.

"The Rukh is the most beautiful bird in the world. Her every feather is made of wisdom and love. Solomon's servants caught her baby in a brass pot and covered it with impenetrable glass. When the mother Rukh saw her child beneath the glass, she threw herself against it with the greatest force. But her body alone could not break it. So, the bird traveled by the force of her love to the bottom of the dark mountain to ask Asmodeus for the Wonderworm. The King of Demons respected a mother's love and gave it to her. With the Shomir she sliced the sliceless glass and freed her child.

"Then Solomon told her why he had captured her baby and described the Temple he would build. The Rukh gave him the Shomir, and the King gave it to his builders.

"From that day forth King Solomon and all his people understood the power of love to break through anything. So, the Great Temple was finished. It was covered with gold and was said to be like a prayer itself. All who saw it were close to God. Then the King himself gave the Shomir back to Asmodeus, who hid it deep in the ocean."

Jana's mother leaned forward. "When I was little you told me that the Wonderworm made no noise as it carved the Holy Temple."

"Oy. Am I getting old. I almost forgot that part. Yes. It was silent. But some say that the silence could be heard." Everyone laughed and finished their dinner.

That night Jana dreamed that a small clay bird which she found in the candy store around the corner came to life in her hand and flew down the street.

The dark mountain within her grew smaller. Sometimes she heard a little girl weeping in the distance, but she did not know where the sound came from.

That summer her family went on vacation to the Adirondacks. A terrible accident almost occurred. A man dove from his boat into the deepest part of the lake and hit his leg on a stone. When he surfaced, he screamed for help. Jana, who was standing alone close to the shore, heard his screams and felt terror. She stood without moving or calling for help. Her brother, who was farther down the beach, also heard the drowning man and ran for assistance. As the man was brought to the shore, Jana heard someone say, "In another minute he would have gone under."

Jana heard the words as if she were waking from a deep sleep. She understood that she had been frozen with fear. She told herself, "I should have saved him. I should have called for help. It is my fault that he nearly drowned."

The mountain grew immense inside her. Her parents came to find her, and she asked to be left alone. They understood. Her brother said under his breath, "It was your fault."

She said to herself, "I am badluck."

Instead of going home, Jana ran as fast as she could. She ran toward the forest to a cave where earlier that week she and her brother had tried to scare each other with spooky tales about what might lurk within. They were unable to enter the darkness. Now, Jana went into the cave. The night of the cave, well hidden from the summer sun, felt safe.

She dug the flashlight from her bookbag and shone light on the walls: gray stones, moist. It was creepy. But she was glad to be there. "I am badluck and this box is just a box and the story is just a story. How can a grandmother in the Bronx have a Wonderworm like King Solomon's!" Defiantly, Jana took the box and broke open the little silver latch. The lid snapped open.

In the light she saw a translucent green copper egg on a faded red velvet cloth. She lifted the egg close to the flashlight. She could make out another egg shape within it, just as her grandmother had described. It felt alive. It moved. Terrified, Jana dropped the flashlight. Darkness engulfed her.

She heard a strange sound: humming—no, moaning. As if someone had turned up a radio too loud, then covered it with blankets. Jana felt too tired to stand. She sank to her knees, careful not to drop the egg. She whispered to herself, "It was just a story. Grandma always tells us stories."

On the cold ground in the cave, she could not help thinking of the Temple of Solomon. She felt as if a stone palace covered with gold was hidden in the darkest place within herself. The egg glowed in her hand. It was as green as an emerald, as blue as the sky. "What if there is a worm inside?" she asked herself, and her hands began to shake.

Jana crouched close to the earth and tried to find the flashlight again, but a tiny sound came from the egg. It was the sound of a child weeping. She held the egg against her heart to comfort it. The weeping became a song.

All that happened after this might be consid-

ered a dream, because it happened in a different way from anything she had known in her life or even in a story.

The green egg that shone in her hands began to grow. At first she saw a winged worm. Then it transformed into a tiny red lizard. Then it turned green, then gold, then white. Its ruby eyes glowed in the dark. Jana was no longer afraid.

Suddenly, it shrank, smaller and smaller, to the size of a tiny, blazing, blue wire of light. She saw the worm. It crawled from her hand along her arm. Jana thought she should scream. She hated worms, but the cool, moist feeling of the worm was comfortable.

The Shomir, for she had no doubt that it was the Wonderworm, slithered up her arm, up her neck, and crept into her ear. It tickled, then stung. Then it was quiet. She was a bottle with a cork that was tight. Jana dared not move.

The song was inside Jana's head. The little creature moved through her. She could feel it gliding through every part of her body. She began to cry. A sorrow so deep and so old that she knew it had to be more than her own filled her. She lay down because her legs could not hold her. The song lulled her to sleep as the worm crawled through her heart. Unknown to Jana, she wept tears of gold.

In the time that she slept, the worm walked

through her with its tiny diamond legs. It did not cut her. She had no dreams or thoughts that she remembered. It was time not counted in this world.

As she awoke, Jana recalled the image of a dark mountain melting.

She sat up, her heart pounding, and found the flashlight. She was in the cave. The cedar box was open on the ground. The little green copper egg had rolled away. She picked it up and shook it. The egg within the egg jiggled like a pebble in a cup.

A cool wind blew through the mouth of the cave. She saw that it was nearly dark outside. "I'd better go home." She placed the egg back in the box and closed the silver latch.

A firefly flickered here and there. Jana turned off the flashlight and followed the firefly out of the cave. She saw her brother walking up the hillside.

"There you are, Jana. Everyone is looking for you, especially me. I am sorry I said what I said. It really wasn't your fault."

"I felt very bad," she said softly as they walked side by side back to the summer house.

During the days that followed, Jana thought about the box, but did not speak about what had happened. She stayed close to home, helping her mother in the garden. She was quiet until her grandmother came to visit for the weekend.

When Jana was finally alone with Malka, in her bedroom, she was struck by how white and thin her grandmother's hair had become. Her skin was like crumpled paper. *She is a very old woman,* thought Jana.

But when Malka tucked her in, the girl saw another face under the old woman's skin: a young face. She saw a girl not more than sixteen, with blue eyes and smooth skin, with thick black braids that hung to her waist.

Surprised by the trick of her eyes, Jana started talking full speed about everything: the drowning man, the cave, the worm, and the singing. The young face smiled and Jana grew still and smiled back. Malka said, "Shh. Go to sleep."

Jana asked her grandmother for a "granny kiss," just the way she did in the Bronx. The old woman held Jana's cheeks with both hands and kissed her forehead, saying, "My beautiful granddaughter. I have given you my gift."

Jana said, "The box is under the bed."

"Good. I don't want you should lose it." Malka smiled knowingly.

The next afternoon Jana walked with her grandmother. They went to see a neighbor's horse, Brownie. Jana ran ahead as the old woman walked slowly behind.

As soon as Brownie saw Jana, he moved toward the fence. He shivered with delight as she touched his nose. Jana ran her fingers over his face and heard a small sound. It was the singing. Then she saw the horse's other body, the one made of light, the way she had seen her grandmother's girl-face. She could see that Brownie was ill.

Then Malka made her way to the fence, her girl-face glowing. Slowly, she stretched her old hands and placed them on the horse's neck behind his ears. Brownie bent toward her, mewing like a kitten. Then he shuddered and turned, pawing the ground. The horse lifted his head proudly, nudged Malka, and raced away. He was no longer ill.

The old woman touched Jana's arm. "What are you looking at?"

Jana knew better than to ask any questions. It was not needed. For the rest of the summer, whenever the old woman visited she taught Jana more and more about how to use the power of the Wonderworm. They never spoke about it directly.

"You bring good luck," exclaimed the old woman.

In the early autumn, back in the city, when the leaves in Malka's garden were beginning to change color, the old woman grew weaker. By the end of September she was gone.

For several weeks following her grandmother's death, Jana helped her mother to clean out the closets and sort through books and boxes of photos to take back to Brooklyn. Jana got to keep the necklace, the blue glass bead, and the silver hand with Hebrew letters. Her mother kept only the copper gypsy amulet.

Jana didn't mention the box to her mother, yet an odd thing occurred at Malka's house. Jana cut her leg on a nail near the closet. She looked at it and it stopped bleeding instantly. Her mother saw this and said, "So Grandma gave *you* the gift."

"What?" asked Jana.

"She gave you the gift," her mother said again. "She wanted to give it to me, but it wasn't meant for me. That is another story I will gladly tell you someday. She received it in the old country from a famous rabbi. She was told it would go to her child or her child's child. When the people came from the old country, they left everything behind, especially magic and stories. They didn't feel it was wanted here."

"Tell me more," said Jana.

"I don't know that much about the gift. It was barely spoken of when I was growing up, until the war. World War II. I was just married, and your father had to leave to fight in Europe. I lived with Grandma. Many people came to visit. I had no idea what they did, but I knew they came because of the gift. Each person stayed a long time. Sometimes they arrived very sad and left stronger, or happier. Before they left they always gave Grandma presents: cakes, jewelry, blessings. I saw her accept the blue bead and this copper amulet. Often they kissed my head. I think they thought that I had the gift."

Jana's mother spoke softly, eyes filling with tears, smiling. "I am proud of you, Jana. It is said in the old country that the gift is always passed on. And that when the world is in need of magic, the Wonderworm appears. Grandma once told me that in this time the Temple in Jerusalem would not be rebuilt in stone, but carved into the hearts of human beings. You will use it well, my daughter."

What would a book of magic tales be without a little visit from Merlin?

QUESTING MAGIC

Mark A. Garland and Lawrence Schimel

"Mom, can we get a questing beast?" Patrick asked. "It won't make a mess, and I promise to take care of it."

"Questing beasts don't exist, honey. We've been over this before."

"Yes, they do. I saw one today at the bus stop. It was hiding behind the dumpster, but I could still see it peeking around."

Patrick's mother hung the dish towel on the rack and turned to look at him. "You know how your father feels about pets. I'm sorry, but we simply can't have one. He wouldn't allow it. Especially with your grades so low. I thought you promised to get your head out of the clouds."

"But—"

"Try getting passing grades in school again, then think about asking for favors. Now, go wash up; dinner's almost ready. Then you've got *homework* to do."

"They do exist," Patrick muttered to himself as he walked down the hallway to the bathroom. As he passed by the front door, he was sure he saw the questing beast peering in through the narrow window on the left. Patrick raced back to the window and looked out, but it was gone.

As he walked to the bus stop the next morning, Patrick looked for the questing beast again. He didn't see it. He was sure it was a questing beast, though, a creature of magic. It looked just like the illustrations in his King Arthur book.

The book! Patrick looked at his watch. "Three minutes until the bus comes," he muttered to himself, turning to run back home. "Maybe I can make it."

"What are you doing here?" his mother yelled when she heard the door.

"I forgot something," Patrick yelled back, running up the stairs to his room.

Patrick grabbed *King Arthur and the Knights of the Roundtable* from his shelf and stuffed it into his backpack. His book report was tucked into the middle of its pages, among words he'd read countless times. That was the only part of his homework he was sure he'd done a good job with, the only part he loved.

His mother screamed: "The bus! The bus!"

"I'm coming, I'm coming!"

Patrick's mother, in her bathrobe, held the front door open for him as he ran down the steps.

"It better have been important," she scolded a moment later as the bus went by without him. "You have to walk now."

"It was my homework," he said truthfully. *And it* was *important,* he thought. He was off to a bad start, and he had a strange feeling that the rest of the day was going to be even worse.

Patrick was at his locker, picking out the books he'd need for his morning classes, when Warren and Bradley Rushfit came up behind him. He'd gotten to school late, so they hadn't caught him in the main hall. "Give us your lunch money, squirt," Warren said. Patrick moaned softly. Sometimes it was his homework they wanted, which was one reason he often didn't have it to turn in. Other times they just wanted to push him around a little, showing off to the other kids. Lately, they'd thought of the lunch money.

"Now!" Brad said, putting his hand on Patrick's shoulder.

Patrick spun around and dropped all his books—history, reading, and math. They landed on Brad's foot.

Brad jumped back and hopped on his other foot. Warren was laughing so hard he let go of Patrick.

"You're gonna get it for this!" Brad howled.

"I'm sorry," Patrick cried as he tried to slam his locker shut, pick up his books, and start running all at the same time. He was clear of the boys when he realized he didn't have his math book, but he kept on going.

At recess, Patrick sat at the top of the bleachers and watched the other kids playing soccer, girls against boys. The girls were winning. But he had bigger things to worry about. Brad and Warren would be out to get him. They'd be waiting by his locker; they knew he couldn't go home without the rest of his books. If he got any more F's or missed any more homework assignments, he wouldn't have to worry about what Warren and Brad would do to him.

The whole world hates me, Patrick lamented. It really felt that way some days. That was why he'd gotten so interested in reading books about fabled, magical lands, and King Arthur especially. He wanted to live in a world like that, to be a knight, a prince, a sorcerer, or a king. Then he brought home that bad report card. His mother had taken all his books away. Except the Arthur one, his favorite—he'd convinced her he needed that one for his book report.

Patrick pulled *King Arthur* from his backpack and started reading the sections about the questing beast. The one he'd seen looked exactly like the picture on page 443—sort of bearlike, except for the neck and a very large, pointy-eared head.

He felt himself being watched and looked up from his book.

Standing just on the other side of the chain-link fence surrounding the playground was the questing beast, staring back. It lowered its long, snakelike neck and peered at him from between the links in the fence, as if suddenly shy. Patrick put the book back in his pack and eased himself down, bench by bench, so as not to startle the creature. Gently he hoisted the pack onto his shoulders. Then he started toward the fence, still moving almost in slow motion.

He was only about ten yards away when a soccer ball came flying over his head and crashed against the fence. He turned around to yell at whoever had kicked the ball. Before he had the chance to say anything, Cindy called, "Sorry about that. I didn't see you standing there. Can you kick the ball back?"

Patrick turned back to the fence. The

questing beast had already fled. All that was left was the soccer ball, still rolling slightly in the gully. He took a swipe at it and missed, then picked up the ball and threw it at Cindy. He felt like crying again. Would *everything* go wrong today?

The beast was back. All afternoon long, Patrick tried not to look out the window. Each time he did, he would find himself entranced, watching the long, sinuous neck of the questing beast as it observed the class. Patrick wished some of the other kids could see the beast. The green fur looked so soft, like a cat maybe. Or a mink coat. But there was something behind the eyes, something in its close-mouthed grin, that spoke of dread. Or magic.

Didn't anyone else see it?

Twice already he'd been called on, and then chastised not to daydream when he didn't know the answer (and sometimes not even the question itself).

So he tried not to look out the window, forcing himself to watch the teacher's every move, or counting the seconds on the clock. But he always wound up looking out again. And the beast would be there. A wondrous beast from a magical place . . .

"Patrick! When was the Boston Massacre?"

This day is never going to end, Patrick

thought as the cycle repeated itself again. He knew he couldn't go through this tomorrow. He had to know. Today.

As soon as last period let out, Patrick ran, hoping to grab the books he needed to take home from his locker before Warren and Brad got there. It almost worked. But by the time he got the combination right and the locker door open, it was already too late. Brad rounded the corner near the auditorium doors at a dead run, then came Warren right behind him. Patrick managed to dodge them both just as they reached him. He took a breath and launched himself.

He ran straight past two teachers, who shouted at him to quit running, then he heard the other boys getting yelled at. He glanced over his shoulder. They were still behind him when he cleared the main threshold and bolted down the sidewalk away from school. When he finally managed to scurry behind a sagging wooden storage shed, gasping, legs aching, he looked up and there it was.

The beast stood in the middle of the next backyard, maybe thirty feet away. It looked bigger now. Magical things could do that, he guessed. It did not run as Patrick approached, but managed to maintain a constant distance between them, only moving ahead when Pat-

rick took a step, and taking only as many steps as Patrick did. Patrick tried to fake it out by lifting his leg and pretending to move forward, but the beast was not fooled, even though its back was turned. Patrick thought it was almost amused by such tricks.

He decided to change his tactic. Instead of stalking the beast, he simply walked after it at a normal pace. The questing beast was forced into the same pace, which also seemed to amuse it. Where would the beast lead him?

It was a meandering route, turning when Patrick least expected it, along streets he had never been on. They walked around the same block twice in a row, and then the beast went up someone's driveway. It shuffled along the side of the house and turned the corner. Patrick followed and discovered the beast had disappeared into a dead end.

No, there was a hole at the bottom of the fence. Patrick took off his backpack and squeezed through the hole, then pulled the pack through. When he stood up on the other side he saw the questing beast waiting again.

"Lead on," he said aloud. Seeming to understand, the questing beast resumed its pace.

It brought him to a huge field just beyond a churchyard, where a Renaissance Faire was in progress. Patrick lost sight of the beast in the crowd, he was so busy looking around at the people in medieval costumes and the various booths. Patrick wondered if the beast had brought him back in time; the whole field seemed to be a page out of history . . . or fantasy. But there were also many people dressed in normal clothes, and even the performers wore modern-day watches and had zippers in their medieval costumes.

"I can't believe no one told me this was here!" he cried out.

To his right, a man handed a sword back to a vendor who wore wizard's garb. Patrick walked over once the man had gone. All sorts of items littered the table, but the daggers and swords were what caught his attention. "I need one of these," Patrick said aloud to himself, "to take care of Warren and Brad."

"What exactly is your problem?" the vendor asked. "It's perhaps best to try another means of solving it than one of these." He indicated the daggers on his table. Then he handed Patrick the largest of the swords. "Nice, isn't it?"

Patrick looked at the blade. It was notched in a few places, and the edge looked pretty dull. "I suppose, but I would expect the real Excalibur to hold an edge better. This one's pretty worn looking for a supposedly magical blade."

"What did you say?" the vendor asked, raising an eyebrow at him, and suddenly Patrick felt guilty for having insulted his merchandise.

He handed the sword back. "You, on the other hand," he added quickly, "have a great costume. You're Merlin, right?"

The vendor dropped the sword. It clattered to the table, knocking daggers and baubles to the grass.

"What did you say?" the vendor asked, ignoring his fallen wares.

"I said your Merlin costume was very good." Patrick took his backpack off and pulled out *King Arthur*. He flipped through its pages until he came to the right picture. "See? You look just like him."

The vendor looked dubious. Patrick thought he must still be insulted by what he'd said about the sword.

"What is this?" the vendor asked him suddenly, holding up a long brown stick.

"Is this some kind of a test? It's a wand, I think. Plastic. With a little face carved into it."

The vendor's eyebrows went all the way up. "This?"

"A crystal ball . . . with a crack."

"And what of this?"

"A metal statue of a wizard. What's going on?"

"Here." He handed Patrick the wizard statue, which was only about eight inches tall, but weighed quite a bit. "Take this. Tomorrow when you go to school, when the time is right, put it in your locker. Count to thirty and then open your locker again. I believe it will solve your problem with the ones you spoke of."

"Warren and Brad," Patrick said. "But how does it work? And how much is it?" He stared at the figurine in his hands, wondering what it did.

"Just take it."

"I can't do that. Let me give you something for it." Patrick reached into his pockets, but he didn't have any money. "I'm sorry, but I don't feel right just taking it."

Out of the corner of his eye, Patrick saw the questing beast once more, sniffing a candied apple at a booth down the row. He'd almost forgotten that following the questing beast was the reason he had come to the fair in the first place. Patrick turned to ask Merlin about the beast, but Merlin was gone, slipped into the crowd. Patrick looked down at the statue in his hands. "I never even got to say thank you," he mumbled.

Turning the other way, he found that the questing beast was gone as well.

Patrick didn't feel like staying at the fair anymore. His mom was going to yell at him for coming home late, and for not having his schoolbooks for homework.

He looked down at the statue in his hands. He didn't see how it could help, but he would do as the man had told him, if only as a favor for the gift.

* * *

At school the next morning, Patrick was counting to thirty, as the man had instructed, when he saw Warren and Brad come around the corner. *Hurry!* he thought, and began to count more quickly. *Twenty-two, twenty-three . . .* Brad and Warren were getting closer. He couldn't wait any longer. He turned the lock and opened his locker for the second time, then blinked against a sudden blinding light. He fell backward, and after a moment felt hands on him, helping him to his feet.

"What happened?" Patrick asked, rubbing his eyes.

"I brought you back to Camelot," a voice said.

Patrick's eyes flew open. He was in a small stone tower instead of a hallway at school with rows of lockers. He was being helped up by the vendor from the fair.

"Excuse me?" Patrick asked.

"I brought you back to Camelot. We haven't much time. Arthur is meeting us. I'll explain everything as we go, but first, put this on." He handed Patrick a dark cape.

Patrick had no idea what was going on. But, as weird as things were, he was finally having an adventure. The easiest thing to do, then, was just to go along and try to figure things out later.

And, if he truly was in Camelot, that meant Warren and Brad were still back in school. He was safe, for the moment at least. The statue had worked after all, in its way.

Patrick threw the cape over his shoulders. It was woven of wool and made his neck itch.

"You'll get used to it," the vendor said, pulling the cloak tightly around Patrick. "Your own clothes would look completely out of place here."

Patrick looked at the soft silk of the wizard's clothes and thought about how easy it was for him to say that he'd get used to it. But all he said out loud was, "Who are you?"

"Merlin. I thought you knew when you saw through my spell. I was very surprised when you did that, though I shouldn't have been. It was then that I knew you were the one I'd sent the beast to look for."

"The questing beast?" Patrick asked.

"You were his quest," Merlin answered. "Now, come along. You are the key to all our problems, and there is much to be done." Merlin opened the one door in the room, revealing a long set of steps.

Saw through my spell . . . The key to all our problems . . . Everything was going too fast for Patrick to follow along. "What problems?" he asked as they descended. "I mean, I'd like to help if I can, but I don't really think—"

"It's the stone. Arthur can't pull the sword from the stone because Morgan Le Fay has put a spell on the area and he can't reach it. That's why we need you."

Patrick paused. It was every dream he could possibly have, all coming true at once, yet it seemed all wrong. "What are you talking about?" He realized he was shouting and lowered his voice. "I mean, how am I supposed to help? The spell is there to keep him out because only the rightful king of England can draw the sword. I'm not the rightful king of England." Patrick stopped himself for a moment. "Am I?" he whispered.

"Of course you're not," Merlin snapped. "Keep moving. I told you I'd explain things as I went."

They began walking down the steps again, Patrick eager for Merlin's explanation.

"We need you because you negate magic."

"What?" Patrick said, halting again.

"You negate magic. Stop it. Make it go away. It's a rare gift, but you have it. That's why you saw through my spell at the Faire. And also through the glamours on some of the objects I had for sale."

Patrick thought for a moment. "But if I negate magic, then how did you bring me here?"

"Oh. That was a tricky one for me, too. I used my magic to go into the future and bring back a small space-time machine, and since that's science, it could work on you without your negating it. I put the time machine inside the figurine, which you put in your locker; it was set to go off when you reopened your locker door. Now, keep walking."

Merlin began walking down the stairs again, and Patrick hurried to keep up with him. "A wizard who uses a time machine?" Patrick mused aloud.

"I am good, aren't I?" Merlin replied as they reached the bottom. They stepped through a doorway, and out onto an ancient, cobbled street with stone houses and pigs in the yard nearest him. Merlin did not even hesitate. "Try to keep up," he said.

They went to the end of the way, then up another street, then quickly around a corner, where Merlin finally stopped in a little square, a place deserted but for a few stray chickens that pecked at the ground near a great gray stone with something sticking out of it.

"My lord," Merlin said.

Patrick turned and saw a young man, someone who looked like he imagined himself when he closed his eyes.

"Arthur?" Patrick managed to ask.

"You are the one Merlin spoke of?" Arthur asked in reply. "The one with the power?"

Patrick took a breath. "I—"

"He is," Merlin answered.

"Then walk with me," Arthur said. A crowd

was gathering, filing into the square behind the young prince, all with eager faces. Arthur paused when he reached the rail fence surrounding the stone. "I've been here many times," he said. "Alone."

Patrick said nothing at all. He was suddenly aware of what was bothering him, and he was stunned by the idea.

"What's wrong?" Arthur asked.

Patrick shook his head. "I wanted nothing more than to be here, to meet you, to be part of the magic. Yet it seems the only reason it's actually happened is that I'm not part of it at all, that I will never be, never could be. My luck is certainly as rotten as ever."

"You don't see it, do you?" Arthur asked. "Where you are, there is only what's real, and where his kind are"—he nodded toward Merlin—"there is mostly what's not. You are each just as important. Magic can't exist without reality, and reality needs a little magic."

Of course, Patrick thought, suddenly seeing the whole thing. He looked over the fence and knew exactly what Arthur was talking about.

"Now, I must have that sword," Arthur said, "but Le Fay's magic keeps me from it. The spell is unbreakable, even for Merlin."

"I have a similar problem with my locker." Patrick sighed. He held out his hand to the once and future king, and they stepped over the fence together. The air seemed to shimmer momentarily, then they walked straight to the stone.

Arthur scrambled up on top of the rock and wrapped both hands around the sword's hilt. Slowly, so slowly Patrick was afraid he hadn't helped after all, the sword came out of the stone. Patrick pressed his hands harder against the stone, and the sword, at last, came free. Arthur lifted Excalibur over his head to the crowd's enthusiastic cheers.

Patrick closed his eyes and imagined, for a moment, that they were cheering for him. He raised his arm above his head. The clasp on his cape came loose, and he opened his eyes as it fell away. He was back at school in front of his locker.

Patrick spun around and came face-to-face— or face-to-back, actually—with Warren and Brad. The two brothers were staring toward the foyer by the auditorium. The questing beast had returned and apparently was visible to them now. It looked nothing like the last time Patrick had seen it: its huge black eyes were wild, and its teeth—long, jagged, and many— were all showing. It bobbed its long dark neck this way, then that, which made a sound like snapping bone and cartilage.

Warren and Brad stepped back until they were cowering behind Patrick. The beast drew nearer, raking the air with its claws. Brad screamed, while Warren sank shaking to his knees. At least a dozen other students were on hand, crouched along the wall where the hallway ended in a pair of locked glass doors. The beast was maybe ten yards away now. . . .

Patrick looked at Warren, then Brad. "You two are pathetic," he said. Then he took two steps forward. The beast took two steps back. It was their same game, but now Patrick knew the reason: it was the only choice the magical creature had if it wished to survive in his magic-negating presence.

Patrick jogged toward the beast and it beat a hasty retreat. People were cheering as Patrick walked back toward them. Warren and Brad still stared down the hallway, as if the beast might suddenly return. They were crying.

It was truly . . . magical, Patrick thought. He got the books he needed, then closed his locker and headed for class.

I usually like big, spectacular magic. But sometimes all that's really needed is just a gentle touch of the stuff.

VISIONS

Sherwood Smith

We'd just stepped off the school bus and were starting up the long hill toward home. We passed a couple of old storefronts and had reached the vacant lot when all four of us saw a flash of gold in the gutter right below our feet.

"Hey!" Lissa exclaimed on one side of me.

"What's that?" Nikki yelled on the other.

I crouched down on the edge of the curb, poking at the trash the rain had piled up in the gutter. In the midst of the withered leaves and soggy papers and mud gleamed a roundish thing, kind of like an extra-large gold coin. As the other three watched, I picked it up and brushed it off.

"What is it, Margo, a badge or something?" Pat asked.

"I don't know, but I like it," I said. Sunlight glanced down between a couple of clouds and made the object glitter and shine so it looked like liquid flame in my hand. It would be great in my collection of Weird Things, I decided—if no one else wanted it.

"It's pretty," Lissa said, touching it daintily. "I wonder who lost it?"

"Is that carving on it?" Nikki pushed her curly black hair out of her eyes as she peered down at my hand. "It looks like something is written on it."

"No, it's leaves," Lissa said, setting her backpack on the sidewalk and bending over my hand.

I tipped my palm so everyone could see the thing. The glitter was so bright it almost hurt my eyes.

Lissa gasped. "There *are* words on it! Look . . . it's kind of old-fashioned, but I can read it. Here's an 'I,' and there's 'molder'—"

"Holder," Nikki said. She grabbed my fingers in her strong brown hand, staring down at the talisman, then up at us, a funny look on her round face. "It says, 'I grant the holder one wish.' "

"Whoa," I said, feeling kind of like little electrical shocks were zinging through my entire body. Had I, Margo O'Toole, found real magic at last? "Lemme see—" Nikki let go of my hand and I nearly smacked myself in the face. "You're right," I said, examining the fancy letters, which looked like something from a fairy-tale book.

"D'you think it's real?" Nikki asked, rubbing her hands.

"No way," Pat said, crossing her arms. "Toss it. It's all gross with mud and gunk, so it's probably crawling with germs."

"If you do, it's mine," Nikki said. "In fact, didn't I see it first?"

"We all saw it at the same time," Lissa said quickly, flinging her blond braids over her shoulders. "You know we did. Margo just picked it up first."

Nikki grinned at me. "But if you don't want it—"

"Who said I didn't want it?" I retorted quickly. "That was Pat."

Everyone looked at Pat. All four of us girls are the same age, and we live on the same block in a not-so-safe part of the city. We've been going back and forth from school together for several years, because we aren't allowed to go alone. Pat's the tallest, and sometimes it feels like she's the oldest. Her lips were pressed together in a familiar line, and her dark eyes were, well, *austere.*

"You guys, it's not going to work. Let's go

home before we get into trouble," Pat said. She sent a worried look up the street.

"Just a sec." I turned it over in my hand. "Well, it's not like there's a name or address on it. I say finders keepers."

"We can make a wish and *then* throw it away," Lissa said, adding to me, "And after that, you can wash your hands."

"Forget it," Pat said, her voice sharp. "I can't believe you're messing with that thing at all."

Nikki and Lissa gaped at her as though she'd turned into a monster. I could see what they were thinking: was this really good old Pat, who was always so quiet, and fair, and so kind she couldn't even step on bugs? I knew she hated any mention of magic these days, but I couldn't tell them that.

"So, if we only get one wish," Nikki said, "we'd better think a little."

"If it's even real," I said, sneaking a look at Pat.

It didn't help. "I can't believe you dummies," she muttered, and turned away. Stalking in the direction of a charred old tree stump right in the middle of the weed-choked lot, she yelled, "I'll get started on my homework while you waste your time."

We all watched her march through the wet weeds, drop down onto the tree stump, and yank her notebook out of her backpack. Lissa and Nikki turned back to me and shrugged, looking down at the talisman. Nikki's brow puckered, and Lissa threw her braids back. "What do you think? Should we wish for a thousand wishes?" she suggested.

"I've never read a story where that worked," I said. "The magic might just split up a thousand ways and you'll get a little of each wish—like just the front porch if you wish for a mansion, or if you want a really cool pair of shoes, you'll wind up with half a shoelace."

Nikki gave a loud snort. "That's one thing I really hate—those stupid stories where the person is granted a wish, and goes for something that seems perfectly okay, but then it turns out to be a total disaster."

Lissa bit her lip, and did a little ballet hop, backing away. "You think that thing is going to zap us? It was in the gutter, after all. Maybe it zapped someone else."

I thought over all the magic stories I'd ever read—and I've read a lot. "Someone might have tossed it," I said, "but then maybe, after it grants its wish, it might just kind of jump into space and land anywhere."

"That's one big jump, Margo," Nikki said, a sour grin on her face as she looked around at the familiar run-down apartment buildings and crummy old stores. "I haven't heard of any sudden millionaires in *this* neighborhood."

"Is that what we should wish?" Lissa asked. "For a million bucks?"

"Or a billion?" Nikki added, closing her eyes.

For about ten seconds, it felt great. I thought about my mom and me getting away from our dinky apartment and buying a house with my share of the money. A mansion! With an entire theme park in the yard. And a limousine—for each of us.

Then I thought about what would happen if we couldn't prove how we'd gotten the money. "I wonder if the IRS would believe us," I said. "The FBI sure won't."

"Who says the IRS would have to know?" Lissa demanded. "We'll keep it a secret, of course."

"Margo's right." Nikki threw her backpack down next to Lissa's and rubbed her chin thoughtfully. "Anybody who suddenly spends big amounts of money gets investigated by nosy tax agents. I've seen it in a million detective shows. They'll think we're with some kind of creepy gang."

"We won't spend big amounts," Lissa said, turning a pirouette. She stopped and sighed. "But then, even if we spend tiny amounts, we'll get investigated by nosy families. At least, I sure will."

"Me, too," Nikki grumped. "Heck—I buy a

candy bar, and my mom wants to know why the money didn't go into my college fund."

I closed my fingers over the talisman. "I'm just wondering if each of us might get a wish," I said. "I mean, if I wish, then hand it off to you, Nikki—you'd be the new holder. Then to Lissa." I was thinking, *And if it really works, we could give it to Pat.*

"But it might disappear," Nikki said, toeing the trash in the gutter, as if another talisman might be uncovered. A car hissed by along the wet street and Nikki jumped back from the splash.

"Let's agree on the first wish," Lissa said. "If it stays, then we agree on the other wishes."

"Fair's fair," Nikki said, kicking mud off her shoe.

"Okay," I said. "So what'll it be?"

"A mansion, maybe?" Nikki threw her arms wide. "Everyone has her own room. No, two rooms. Five! A bathtub like a swimming pool for each!"

Lissa closed her eyes and sighed. I grinned, thinking again of royal palaces with rooms and rooms of fun stuff to do.

But then Nikki snorted again and said, "Wait a minute. It's only *one* wish, geeks."

"What?" Lissa exclaimed.

"We have one wish," Nikki repeated, looking from one of us to the other, her brown eyes wary. "If we wish for a palace, we might get one, but I bet it doesn't come with furniture. And even if it did"—she made a terrible face—"who's going to clean up a million rooms? Not me! It's bad enough being stuck with cleaning our little place when my mom's too tired."

"And who's going to let a kid keep a palace in the middle of the city?" Lissa said, shrugging her shoulders.

I groaned. "I can't think of anything that won't backfire. Like, if we wish for an unending supply of ice cream—"

"We end up ralphing at the sight of it," Lissa finished. "I just thought of that as well."

We stared at each other.

"Maybe we could fix things in our lives," Nikki said slowly. "All four of us have had divorces happen in our families. Maybe it would work for all of us—even Pat—if we wished our parents were back together again, and all happy."

We looked at each other. Lissa turned another slow pirouette, then faced Nikki. "I hate to say it, but do you really *want* your dad back?"

Nikki's head dropped and her hair swung forward and covered her face. I couldn't see her eyes, but I didn't have to. The few times her dad had visited, it always ended up with him getting drunk, and though Nikki never complained in front of me, I think her dad was pretty mean to Nikki and her brothers and sisters.

She looked up. "I don't, but my mom might. At least, she'd like another paycheck, or the child support he owes us, or *something.*"

Lissa said, "I like my stepparents now. If the magic brought my parents together again, what would happen to my half-brother, Sean, since his father is my stepdad . . . and how about the new baby my stepmom is expecting?"

I'd been thinking while they talked, and I said, "In the stories, forcing a change onto someone else's life always turns out rotten. Even if you did it for the best reasons."

"It would be a good thing in Pat's family," Nikki said seriously. "I mean, except for my dad, who's just a flake, at least all our parents want us. Hers don't even want her anymore—and that aunt of hers is mean. She just treats her like a maid and a babysitter."

"Which makes it extra rotten," Lissa added, "because there's no one in the world who works harder, at school or home, than Pat."

"Or is more fair to other people."

"I just don't see why she's so mad," Lissa added, looking at Pat on her tree stump.

I opened my hand again and stared down at the talisman, thinking hard. Pat and I lived next door to each other, so we'd spent a lot of time together. When we were little we mostly acted out the adventure stories we read and loved. I'd started collecting Weird Things in first grade, and Pat used to help me—we always hoped one of them would turn out to be left by aliens, or would transport us to another world. Then the problems started at Pat's home, and trying to test the magic from books to see if it was real turned from a game into a kind of quest.

Lissa and Nikki knew about my Weird Things collection, but not about this. I thought about how in fourth grade Pat and I used to run into thick fog banks, hoping they'd turn out to be a magic gateway to Middle Earth, and how we tried to open the backs of our closets to see if we could get to Narnia.

Once we tried a love potion on her parents. That was before both of them left and her grandmother moved in. Pat's grandmother really loved her, but after only a year she died, and Pat's aunt moved in—with her kids. Pat's life was now exactly like Cinderella's—except there was no fairy godmother, and Pat no longer believed in magic.

I looked over at her, sitting on the stump, crouched over her math book. I couldn't see her face, but her bony shoulders looked fierce. *That's why she's angry,* I thought. *It'll hurt too much if this thing doesn't work.*

But I couldn't say anything—I knew she'd hate it if I talked about all our tries to get to Narnia and Oz. I turned back to Nikki and Lissa.

"We can't bring her grandma back to life," I said.

Nikki made a face. "Yeah, Margo's right. She might come back as a zombie."

"Eeeeeugh," Lissa and I said together, exchanging gross-out looks.

"But if her parents were together again, and loved her . . . ?" Lissa said.

My mind was racing now. "Would it really work, though?"

"What do you mean?" Lissa and Nikki exclaimed at the same time. They grinned at each other, then turned to me expectantly. Another car whooshed by along the rainy street, but this time neither of them noticed the splash.

"Well," I said, "is it right to make people go back to the way they were without asking? I mean, how would you like it if a magic spell forced you to be like you were in first grade?" I asked.

Lissa said slowly, "We're talking about getting them to love Pat again."

"But they don't," Nikki said, frowning. "I think I see it—it'd be fake, wouldn't it?"

"Right," I said. "At least, fake or not, it would be fake for Pat. She'd always know they were back together because of the spell, not for her. Or even for each other."

"I see," Lissa said. "They might not even act real, but like programmed dolls, or something, if we force them to change." She stuck out her tongue. "Heck, there's always a chance this won't even work in the first place," she went on, pointing to the talisman in my hand. "Will it really matter to us if it doesn't?"

Again we looked at each other. "Not to me," Nikki said, smacking her hands together. "I got my life planned out. College, law school, then goin' after corporate pirates."

Lissa whispered, "If it were just mine, I might have wished that I'd get a scholarship to a good ballet school—except then I'd have to worry that I was good enough once I got there."

"You want to wish you would be the best dancer in the world?" I asked.

Lissa's whole body tensed as she closed her eyes, then she said, "No. It's like what you said about Pat—I'd always know the applause was for the talisman, and not for me. I'd hate that."

"So what do we do," I asked, "throw it away?"

"There's a chance it's real," Nikki said.

"I know," Lissa said. "I'm just wondering if we could ask Pat if there's something she would want."

"And get our noses bitten off?" Nikki said, grinning. "She already let us know pretty clearly that she thought this whole thing was stupid."

They both turned to me. "She wouldn't touch the talisman," I said, "though she's the one who needs it most."

"So what do we do?" Lissa asked. "We can't change her life for her, and she won't take the thing and do it herself."

I said, "Maybe we can't send her to the ball, but we could give her a glass slipper."

"What?" Nikki asked, making one of her faces.

Lissa's eyes went wide, and she laughed. "I know what you mean," she said, and did a little dance step on the sidewalk. "When Cinderella had that slipper, it was her proof that magic had happened. We could give Pat hope. I mean, if magic is real just once, then it could happen again."

"Anything could happen," I said, thinking of all the stories I'd read—and all the ones I hoped to act out someday, on the stage.

"She might even start looking for it," Nikki said, nodding slowly.

"So we're all in favor?" I asked.

Lissa smiled, making a graceful dancer's bow, and Nikki smacked her hands together. "Do it, Margo."

I raised the talisman, the other two reached up to touch it as well, and I said, "We wish Pat would see magic."

Then we turned to face Pat, not knowing what—if anything—to expect.

For a moment, nothing happened.

Then Pat's head came up, and she looked at us. It was a long look, an odd look, as if she saw something else besides us. I felt a weird tingling in my bones, and around the edges of my vision light flickered, like tiny stars, but I didn't dare move or even turn my head.

For a long time we all just stood there, and then Pat got up.

And she smiled.

It wasn't a big grin, like Nikki's best, or a giggly smile, like Lissa's when she's feeling silly. It was a little one, but it glowed in her eyes and her cheeks and her forehead—it made her all bright for a moment.

She picked up her books and came down the hill, still smiling.

I looked down at my empty hands: the talisman had disappeared. It didn't matter, I realized as I stooped to pick up my backpack. It didn't matter because we'd each gotten a gift after all. We'd given Pat her glass slipper, and the look in her face gave it right back.

"C'mon," I said, laughing, as I looked at the others. "Let's go, or we'll be late for the ball."

ABOUT THE AUTHORS

JANE YOLEN has published over a hundred and fifty books. Her work ranges from the slap-happy adventures of Commander Toad to such dark and serious stories as *The Devil's Arithmetic* to the space fantasy of her much-beloved "Pit Dragon Trilogy." She lives in a huge old farmhouse in western Massachusetts with her husband, computer scientist David Stemple.

LAWRENCE WATT-EVANS is the author of about two dozen novels of science fiction, fantasy, and horror, and about five dozen short stories. "Horsing Around" is his fourth story in this series of anthologies. He lives in Maryland with his wife, two kids, two cats, two hamsters, and a parakeet named Robin.

JANNI LEE SIMNER grew up on Long Island and has been working her way west ever since. She currently lives in Tucson, Arizona, where she enjoys hiking and horseback riding in the mountains that surround the city. She's published over a dozen short stories—including contributions to *Starfarer's Dozen* and *Bruce*

Coville's Book of Nightmares—and *Phantom Rider*, a series of novels for middle-grade readers.

JESSICA AMANDA SALMONSON is a recipient of the World Fantasy Award, the Lambda Award, and the ReaderCon Award. She's published a half-dozen novels and a gazillion short stories and poems over the last twenty years, ending up in numerous "year's best" anthologies. Her novelette, "Namer of Beasts, Maker of Souls," was published as part of *The Merlin Chronicles*. She lives in Seattle.

NINA KIRIKI HOFFMAN's short fiction has appeared in many magazines and anthologies, including *Bruce Coville's Book of Aliens*. Her book *The Thread That Binds the Bones* won a Bram Stoker Award for first novel. Her second novel is *The Silent Strength of Stones*. She lives with many cats and has a witchball in her backyard.

NANCY SPRINGER is the author of twenty-nine books for adults, children, and young adults, including the 1995 Edgar Award winner in the young adult category, *Toughing It*. Her most recent novel for young adults is *Looking for Jamie Bridger*. Her fantasy novel *Larque on the Wing* was the 1995 co-winner of the James

Tiptree, Jr., Award. A resident of Dallastown, Pennsylvania, she enjoys writing poetry as well as fantasy and realistic fiction, and when not writing can often be found horseback riding.

LAURA SIMMS is one of the foremost storytellers in the world. She is also an award-winning author and recording artist. Her most recent children's books are *Moon and Otter and Frog* and *Rotten Teeth.* She has recorded a CD of *Tales About Water* with musicians Jorge Alfano and Randy Crafton. She lives in New York and travels the world telling stories and teaching storytelling.

MARK A. GARLAND read a copy of Arthur C. Clarke's "The Sands of Mars" when he was twelve and proceeded to exhaust the local library's supply of science fiction. Eventually he tried writing short stories of his own, but got sidetracked into working as a rock musician and a race car driver. Finally he came back to science fiction and has published three novels and over two dozen short stories. He now lives in upstate New York with his wife (also an avid reader), their three children, and (of course) a cat.

LAWRENCE SCHIMEL has written short stories and poems for over sixty anthologies, including *Phantoms of the Night, Weird Tales from Shakespeare, Orphans of the Night,* and many others. He grew up on a horse farm with all sorts of animals—llamas, ferrets, goats, quail (and, of course, horses!)—and now lives in Manhattan, where he translates comic books from Spanish to English and works in a children's bookstore.

SHERWOOD SMITH lives in California. She began making books out of paper towels when she was five—usually stories about flying children. She started writing about another world when she was eight and hasn't stopped since. She has stories in several anthologies, including others in this series, and has published three fantasy novels for young readers: *Wren to the Rescue, Wren's Quest,* and *Wren's War.*

JOHN PIERARD, illustrator, lives with his dogs in a dark house at the northernmost tip of Manhattan. *Bruce Coville's Book of Magic* is the sixth anthology he has illustrated in this series. His pictures can also be found in the *My Teacher Is an Alien* quartet, in the popular *My Babysitter Is a Vampire* series, in the *Time Machine* books, and in *Isaac Asimov's Science Fiction Magazine.*

Photo: Jules

BRUCE COVILLE was born in Syracuse, New York, and grew up in farm territory not far north of that city. He first fell under the spell of writing when he was in sixth grade and his teacher gave the class an extended period of time to work on a short story.

Sixteen years later—after stints as a toymaker, a gravedigger and an elementary school teacher—he published *The Foolish Giant*, a picture book illustrated by his wife and frequent collaborator, Katherine Coville. Since then Bruce has published nearly fifty books for young readers. Many of them, such as *Into the Land of the Unicorns, Jennifer Murdley's Toad,* and *Goblins in the Castle,* are filled with magical events.

These days Bruce and Katherine live in an old brick house in Syracuse, along with their youngest child, Adam, and their cats Spike, Thunder, and Ozma.